Greed Part 1

Gotham Books

30 N Gould St.
Ste. 20820, Sheridan, WY 82801
https://gothambooksinc.com/

Phone: 1 (307) 464-7800

Published by Gotham Books (May 20, 2023)

ISBN: 979-8-88775-292-1 (P)
ISBN: 979-8-88775-293-8 (E)

Table of Content

Chapter 1

I starred at the clock, anxious for my fifth period biology class to end. My teacher Mr. Jones lectured on and on regarding the human body. During his lecture, I fantasized how miraculously my life would change if I was rich. Although me and my brother Cameron were blessed to have a life of riches due to our parent's accomplishments, I wanted my own fortune. I didn't want to leech of my parents' wealth for a lifetime. I knew I needed a business plan and not only that, I also didn't need to work alone. It had to be someone I trusted and apart from my parents, my brother was the only one I trusted.

I always had difficulty staying awake in biology. It wasn't because I had no interest in the subject. It was simply the way he taught. I dreaded every Tuesday and Thursday when I was scheduled to take his class. His voice was always monotoned and it was this very reason no one took him seriously. On days I did stay awake he always called upon me to answer all his questions since my classmates didn't care to. I didn't care either but since I was the smartest in my class and probably in the entire school, I felt I was cursed.

Class ended with Mr. Jones tapping me on my shoulder. I didn't realize everyone already left. He informed me of the homework assignment as I gathered my belongings. I was happy as hell it was the weekend, everything Mr. Jones said went through one ear and out the other. However, on my way out to meet my brother I nodded as if I understood. When I closed his door, my brother startled me from behind. He pissed me off, but I didn't stay angry for long.

We met our parents in front of the school. When inside the car, they greeted us and asked us about our first day of our junior year. My brother answered first. His first day was horrible. He got in three fights and was sent to the principal's office three times. The principle called our parents numerous times during the day but never got a hold of them. Had they had answered our principal Mr. Jenkins, more than likely they would've gotten cursed out.

Our parents shifted their attention towards me when their conversation ended with my brother. I smiled at them then informed them of my series of the series of events that took place from the time they dropped us off at seven that morning until the time we got in the car. My first period was a nightmare. I was assigned to a teacher who spoke very little English. I spent the entire period trying to understand her. I sat with my second period classmates and waited for our teacher to show for forty-five minutes then left. My third through fifth period was a blur.

Before my dad pulled into the driveway he stopped at the mailbox and pulled the mail out. When he parked into the garage, he stopped me and Cameron before we could get out the car. He wanted us to do our homework before we did anything else. I opened my door and cut my brothers response off. I told our father we would have our homework completed in no time, then closed my door. Shortly after Cameron joined me upstairs in my room. He took his backpack off and sat on my binbag.

For a few minutes my brother watched me pace the floor. He became incredibly irritated with me. When ten minutes passed, and I still hadn't said a word he yelled at me. I then became incredibly irritated with him. I told him not to rush me and his response was if he waited for me any longer, he'd be an old man. I laughed then sat beside him, I then proceeded with a question. I asked him what his plan was after high school, he couldn't answer me.

It was crystal clear he hadn't thought that far ahead. After my chat with him his perception of life changed. Mentally and emotionally, he was on board with me of us becoming our own boss someday. Clocking in and out of a shitty job wasn't an option. Cameron leaned back, grabbed the remote controller, and turned on my television. Afterwards he walked down the hall to his bedroom. During his absence I showered and did my homework.

Cameron returned to my room a couple hours later. He showed me a handgun one of his friends purchased online for him. It was beautiful, an all-white nine-millimeter. I gazed upon its beauty as I held it for a few seconds. I then pointed at my mirror and pretended to pull the trigger. I did this five times then handed it back to my brother. I ran for my bed and jumped on it.

I jumped up and down on the bed repeatedly while I checked my brother's homework. We were total opposites on the intelligence spectrum. Most times I did my brothers assignments just so he could pass all his classes. Sometimes it was mind boggling but he was my brother and I wanted to see him graduate. As I suspected all his answers were incorrect. I corrected his answers then handed him his homework. He placed it in his backpack then walked towards my doorway, on his way out he told me after school the next day he wanted to introduce me to two of his friends.

I laid in my bed to get some shut eye. When I turned my lamp off my father entered my bedroom. When I heard his voice, I leaned to my left and turned my lamp back on. When I focused my eyes on him, he whispered to me he knew I did my brothers homework. I stared at him without blinking and denied the allegation. On his way out he demanded I stop. I turned my lamp off again then thought I had been doing Cameron's homework for a while that I didn't know how to stop.

The next morning when our parents dropped us off at school, we were approached by the three guys my brother fought the day before. They forced us into the front door of the school. I was picked on by simply being with my brother at the wrong time, but that didn't matter to me. I wasn't going to allow anyone to bully him. Although we could defend himself, he was outnumbered. He didn't put much effort into the fight, I assumed because it was early in the morning, he was tired. In a blink of an eye, we were pinned to the door with their hands around our neck, I used my right hand and reached into my back pocket.

I stabbed both guys in their eyes with the pen I retrieved from my back pocket. Both let us go when they could no longer see. Me and Cameron grabbed our backpacks and ran into the school. When in front of my first class we hugged then went our separate ways. As soon as I sat in my assigned desk my teacher approached me and mouthed the words five minutes late. I rolled my eyes at her then looked straight ahead. When I got comfortable, she woke me up and sent me to the principal's office.

Principal Jenkins was by far the coolest principle alive in my eyes. Me and my brother were usually sent to his office at least four times a week. When I arrived, principal Jenkins greeted me at the door then invited me inside his office. I sat down while he got us two beers from his mini refrigerator. He threw me a beer as he sat down. After I proposed a toast to wealth, we opened our beers and drank them as fast as we could. I became incredibly dizzy and so did he, but it didn't stop us from drinking more. An hour later I was too drunk to go back to go back to my first period.

I woke up on the floor with my hand in the trash can. I stood up and saw principal Jenkins passed out in his chair with his feet on his desk. Immediately after waking him, he threw up on my all-white air force ones. I was pissed but didn't express it. I figured he suffered enough from the alcohol, and he had an advantage most people didn't. He knew both my parents personally; they grew up together. It was the perfect concoction, no matter how many times me and my brother got in trouble we were untouchable.

It was lunchtime when I sobered up a little. Principal Jenkins wife called and wanted him to come home and have lunch with her. The issue was he still was in no condition to do anything, especially drive. I took it upon myself to take him home, I needed his car for later. I couldn't wait to find out what my brother had planned for the evening. Fifteen minutes later we left the school, and thirty minutes later we arrived at their house. Shortly after I pulled into their driveway, his wife looked out the window then rushed outside to the passenger side.

His wife opened the door, hugged and kissed him. She thanked me for bringing him to her, she knew he was a heavy drinker. She wanted him to stop but she felt she would be on her death bed before that happened. She loved him and no matter what she would never leave him. The love she had for him was beautiful. It was the type of romance I dreamed of, but I had to find the right woman. Every girl I dated was a gold digger.

Principal Jenkins wife Rose helped him out the car. When she closed it, I rolled my window down and asked them if it was alright for me to keep the car until the morning. Instead of them giving me money they decided the car would suite me better. Before I left, I made sure they got inside safely. I then headed back to school. I texted my brother to come outside so he could see the car. Ten minutes later I saw him running towards me.

Cameron was thrilled to see the car. When he asked me whose car it was, I told him principal Jenkins. He was surprised our principal had given me his car so easily. I explained to him what happened and afterwards he understood. We stayed in the car for a few minutes, talked, and smoked a blunt. My brother told me we were going to get some cash before we went home after school. My curiosity was no longer a mystery anymore, I was happy he told me before I exploded.

Me and Cameron walked back in the school. I went to my fourth period class, and he went to his. In my fourth period class I had enemies. They were three sisters who were bullies. Their names were Jennifer, Jessica, and Julie. I hated them with a passion. They bullied me for years. I found out from my brother the reason they hated me was because our father dated their mother and he cheated on her.

When I found out what our father did to their mother, I had to admit it was fucked up, but it wasn't a good enough reason to me for Jennifer, Jessica, and Julie to bully me every day when I never did anything to them. I was fed up; it was the first-time murder was on my mind. They had to pay, all I had to do was think of where and when. They would be tortured prior to their death. I also would make sure I record their death on my camera. Timing was important, I had to snatch them when their guard was down.

I walked in my fourth period with a frown on my face. I didn't want to be there, but I had no choice. There was an empty seat directly in front of the teacher. I walked towards it. Jennifer blew a spit ball at me. I was disgusted it landed on my forehead. I took the spit ball off and sat in the desk.

I was irritated the teacher had given us a lot of homework. I had no intentions to do it. I refused to spend all night doing homework when I had a shitload the night before. When the bell rang, I was the first to leave. I passed Cameron in the hallway, we bumped knuckles and kept moving. Entering my fifth period class, Mr. Jones requested my homework before I could sit down. I huffed and puffed as I reached into my backpack and handed him the assignments.

Mr. Jones gathered all the assignments from everyone then proceeded teaching. The girl I cheated off threw me a note. I opened and it read "one hundred bucks for helping". That was a very fair price and since money wasn't much of an issue for me, I gave her extra. I folded the note with the money in it and threw it back to Kim. She opened it and smiled at me. I then texted my parents and told them they didn't have to pick me and Cameron up from school.

My mother responded; she was relieved they didn't have to come get us. They were relaxing watching movies. I put my cellphone back in my pocket and listened to Mr. Jones as much as I could before class was over. I stared at him, and my eyes became heavy. He was literally putting me to sleep and before I knew it, I was asleep. Luckily, I didn't get in trouble. The bell rang when I opened my eyes.

I waited for my brother at the door of his fifth period class. When he saw me, he began slow jogging towards the front door of the school. For whatever reason I approached the doors with my eyes closed. My brother's crazy ass kicked the doors open. I opened my eyes and ran for principal Jenkins's car. My brother followed. I threw him the keys and we both got inside.

Cameron guided me to two of his friends' houses. We picked them up and Cameron introduced us to each other. His two friends William and Tony seemed to be pretty laid back like myself. We got along perfectly. We drove around for a little while and smoked a couple blunts. During that time Tony told us he had a friend we could rob. I wanted to know more, I asked him why his friend was the perfect target for us.

Tony answered my question. His friend was a local drug dealer who always flashed his money around. Tony was surprised no one attempted to rob him until us. I pulled over and allowed Tony to drive. He drove us to his friend's house. We parked across the street. Tony turned off the car, he then let us know how many people were inside.

We put our heads together and thought of a game plan. Twenty minutes later we had one. The plan was for me to ring the doorbell, when Tonys friend answered Cameron and his friends would hold him at gunpoint and force themselves into the house. Cameron gave us each a Halloween mask. I objected to us using them, they were ugly. My brothers' feelings were hurt but he didn't hold a grudge against me for long. Cameron threw our masks out the window, he then reached into his backpack and gave us a different color stocking cap.

We watched Tonys friend's house for ten minutes before getting out the car. I sensed the others were afraid to go through with the plan, I knew I was. William attempted to get out the car, we stopped him. I confessed my fears and they listened. Anything could go wrong, and we couldn't go through the robbery afraid. We had to be prepared for anything. In the end we decided we couldn't allow our fears to control us.

We got out the car and ran to the house after Cameron lead us in prayer. I was the last to make it to the porch. I stopped to tie my shoes. I took a deep breath, looked to my right and saw Tony, then looked to my left and saw my brother and William. I rang the doorbell, shortly after a woman who appeared to be in her early forties answered. My brother, Tony, and William forced themselves inside. I stood in the doorway paralyzed with fear.

My brother came back for me and pulled me inside the house. While my brother hogtied the individuals who were at the house at that time, I searched for the drugs and money with William and Tony. We ran upstairs and searched the five rooms and found nothing. William and Tony then ran downstairs and continued to search. I stayed upstairs and used the bathroom, while I sat on the toilet, I heard a vehicle pull into the driveway. I hurried and pulled up my pants without wiping myself. I then ran downstairs yelling to warn my brother and his friends.

Cameron and William panicked when they heard music blasting from the strange vehicle they saw in the driveway. Tony recognized the black challenger as his friend car. Tony then panicked along with the others. The older woman managed to break free. She screamed while running for the door. I pulled her back inside and slapped her so hard she fell to the ground unconscious. I starred at the right side of her cheek; my handprint was on her face.

I was weary of going outside, I didn't know what I was walking into. I grabbed the gun my brother had and headed for the front door. I assured him I would handle it. I slowly opened the front door and placed the gun in my right back pocket. I asked one of the guys for his sister's name, he told me Jasmine. I headed towards the black challenger. Halfway there three guns were pointed at me.

It was the first time I had three guns pointed at me. Once again, I stood paralyzed with fear. My brother couldn't save me that time. I thought of something the men would believe. I bravely continued walking towards their vehicle. One guy warned me to stop, if I didn't, they would shoot. I stopped, they wanted to know who I was and why I was there.

I introduced myself as Jasmine's friend. One of the guys called Jasmine's cellphone, she didn't answer. He called her a second time, William answered the phone and pretended to be her. The phone call eased their suspicions. I was allowed to go back inside the house. I smoked a cigarette while I waited in the front yard for, they guys to go inside. Finally, an hour later they went inside.

I followed them into the house. I had a gun pointed in the back of the last guy in line. All three men were greeted by my brother. When they realized our intentions, it was too late for them to run. William and Tony locked all doors and boarded all windows. To the left of them was Jasmines body. Her boyfriend Chico kneeled beside her and cried.

Cameron tied the men up while me, Tony, and William held a gun to their heads. Afterwards, I let them know if they didn't tell us everything we needed to know, they would die where their bodies sat. Chico told us everything, it wasn't long after we had all their dope and all their money. Chicos friends were angry with him for snitching. I figured on our way out we could call us even. My brother, tony, and William took all the duffle bags out the car. On my way out I shot Chico twice in his right leg and twice in his left foot.

Chapter 2

I took all the guns in the house and ran to principal Jenkins's car. I got inside and heard gunshots. Cameron sped off during two girls reloading. He drove as fast as he could until we were home, we lost them. Our parents were home and we had to find a way to get everything inside. Cameron parked the car in the backyard and took everything inside. Meanwhile I walked to the front to distract my parents while William and Tony followed.

I unlocked the front door, and we silently went inside. My parents were in the kitchen preparing dinner. We tried tiptoeing our way upstairs, but my parents caught us. I introduced William and tony as my new friends and that I met them through Cameron. I then added Cameron was out putting gas in principal Jenkins's car and that he would be home soon. My mother smiled at me and told William and Tony they were welcome to stay for dinner if they wanted. On our way upstairs I felt the hairs on the back of my neck stand, I knew my parents knew I lied.

As the night continued, me and Cameron were shocked our parents never addressed the issue. Cameron left all the bags in the hallway upstairs. Tony and William put all the duffle bags into my room and waited there for us to return. Me and Cameron went downstairs and helped our parents in the kitchen to cover our asses. When in the kitchen our father wanted to know what we were up to. We didn't tell them the truth, instead we told them we had a project to do, and William and Tony were our partners. We assumed they accepted our answer, they didn't pry into our business anymore that night.

I yelled for Tony and William to come downstairs; dinner was ready. Tony must've been starving, he damn near broke his neck trying to get to the dining room table. I sat next to my brother, Tony sat next to William, and my father sat across from my mother. Tony and William began stuffing their faces with food. Evidently, they weren't used to having a home cooked meal. My mother stopped them in their tracks. They dropped their forks and the food in their mouths on their plates, at that point dinner was over for me.

Cameron and our father starred at William and Tony while I starred at my plate of food I could no longer eat. The woman of the house expressed to the boys if they wanted a place at our dinner table, they would have to respect us. They both apologized to us, we accepted. My parents then properly introduced themselves to the boys. My father a doctor and my mother a lawyer. After dinner they gave them a tour of the mansion. They loved it so much they wanted to spend the night.

Tonys mother and William's grandpa were called. Both parents had given their approval for them to spend the night with us. They ran upstairs to my room excited to join us. I locked my bedroom door and unzipped one of the four duffle bags. I looked inside and counted the money. My brother and his friends opened their bags and did the same. We each had a total of five grand.

We threw money in the air having a money shower. We then gathered all the bags of marijuana and stashed them in the back of my walk-in closet. We discovered we had over thirty pounds of weed. We had nothing to smoke the weed in. After showering and changing our clothes we went to a gas station up the street from us to buy cigarillos. I pulled up to a gas pump and parked the car. I didn't get out the car right away.

I waited to see who would get out the car. A few minutes later one of the two brothers from the robbery stepped out and looked directly at us. We all ducked, and I started the car. He shot at us while I had the car in reverse. I didn't know how we escaped all those bullets, but once again we were blessed to live another day. The only thing that had several bullet holes was principal Jenkins's car. We didn't have enough time to get it fixed but I figured he would remain calm if I gave him some of our money from the robbery.

Early the next morning before school we ran into trouble when Tonys friend Henry and Henrys friend Keith blocked us in on opposite ends of the street. Principal Jenkins car was already damaged enough, in my eyes nothing could damage it further. Keith was Tonys friend, he was angry we robbed them. Keith tried to make a deal with me. They would let us go if we gave them back everything. I stood up and yelled looking both way through the sunroof of principal Jenkins's car. We pretended to accept the deal.

I sat back down in the car and explained to my brother and his friends what my plan was. My cleverness was appealing to them. I stood up through the sunroof again and yelled "I have everything in my car". They would have to come to me if they wanted it. I sat back down in my seat, and we waited for their move. Keith called Henry and told him to walk to us and get their shit back. Henry was hesitant of course, he asked Keith why he couldn't do it.

Keith and Henry argued for twenty minutes straight. It was by far the longest argument I ever witnessed. Their call ended with Henry slightly opening his door. Everyone starred at Henry to see what he was to do. Five minutes later he stepped out completely and proceeded to walk to us slowly. I told everyone in the car to put their seatbelts on. They were curious to know why.

13

Henry knocked on the drivers' side window when he made it to the car. I rolled it down slowly and he leaned in wanting to know where everything was. I pushed him with the door and got out. He followed me to the trunk. I opened it and all he saw was a quilt. He leaned in and moved it. I turned around and saw Keith still watching from a distance.

When Henry realized there was no money and no drugs he tried to run. I pulled his shirt pulling him back to me. I put him in a choke hold and screamed asking Keith "is this what you fucking wanted to see, huh"?! I then put the gun in Henry's mouth and shot him. His body hit the ground and I proceeded towards Keith's car and shot at him a few times. The last bullet went through his left eye, the seat, and the back windshield. When I got to Keith's car, I looked at the giant hole where his left eye once was.

I hopped in the car through the sunroof. I started the car and drove straight through Henry's car. We arrived at school two hours too late. We smoked a blunt and listened to music for an hour then went inside. William and Tony went to class. Meanwhile me and Cameron went to Principal Jenkins office. He was happy to see us and wanted the keys to his car. We tried to tell him his car was fucked up, but he kept cutting our words off. We gave up on telling him since he wouldn't or couldn't listen, plus it wouldn't be long until he saw it.

We stayed in principal Jenkins's office while he went outside to his car. I sat in his office chair while Cameron sat on his desk. We watched him through his office window. We laughed from far when he saw his car. He screamed and threw a temper tantrum for a while. After so long it was no longer funny. We joined him outside, he was furious and didn't know how he was going to explain the damages to his wife.

Our principal had no idea his wife was the least of his worries. I was certain by then we were all over the news and so was the vehicle. He expressed he was still furious we brought his car back in the condition it was in. My brother got pissed at him and told him we still had classes to attend. A cold death stare from our principal followed my brother's statement. Our principal then expressed how could we get mad at him when we were the ones who fucked up. He had a point, but it didn't matter.

What mattered most was how we were going to move forward. I unzipped my backpack and gave our principal a few thousand dollars. He wanted to know how we got all that money and if there was more. I glanced back at my brother as he walked into school, I assumed to go to class. I turned around and looked at principal Jenkins and said, "open your eyes man." He was left in the parking lot. I wasn't angry with him at all, his curiosity reminded me of innocence.

Principal Jenkins was someone I felt I could control. I sensed he and his wife needed more money. When I was younger, I always thought principals made a lot, but that wasn't the case. Our principal was a prime example. They literally lived in a raggedy mobile home. I was so thankful we weren't invited inside. Had we been invited, more than likely the outcome would've been deadly.

I arrived at my third period class forty-five minutes late. I went inside and nobody was there. I found out by the janitor class was cancelled. I was pissed, I didn't understand why I was assigned to a teacher who obviously didn't have a desire to help the students. I had twenty minutes left until my next class. I stood with my back against the wall, around the corner I heard a familiar voice. I ran around the corner and saw my brother horseplaying with two girls.

The two girls were twin sisters, and they were sexy as hell. The issue was my brother was blinded by their

15

beauty. The girls were bubbleheads, their beauty was the only thing that kept my brother on a leash. Lust was what filled his relationships, he was always searching for a girl to fill an empty void. In the end, most times he was the one with a broken heart. My brother was a giving individual, no doubt about that. He deserved true love, and I hoped one day I would see him fall in love and not only that I hoped he would have a family of his own as I wanted the same.

My fourth period class began, my teacher must've gotten dressed in the dark. She arrived with her hair dyed baby blue. To make matters worse her outfit was a shitty brown. Everyone in the entire school was disgusted with her. Everywhere she went people laughed. I couldn't focus with her looking the way she was looking. I spent the whole period taking pictures of her, when class ended, I uploaded a video of her to YouTube.

During my fifth period I checked the video I uploaded of my teacher. The video had already reached a million views in an hour. Mr. Jones was angry nobody was listening to him. His anger didn't bother us at all, we continued watching the video repeatedly and laughing as loud as we could. Fifteen minutes into his lecture he was interrupted by his wife. He stepped out and closed the door behind him. His wife kissed him, they then walked away from the door.

Mentally many of us were still stuck on that video. I wanted to see it on a bigger screen, I walked to the front of the class and turned on the projector. We saw the video several more times. We were the loudest class in school, but we never got in trouble. Mr. Jones returned with his wife and appeared angrier than before he left. I quickly sat down with a smirk on my face. By the look on his face, I already knew what his response was, he didn't have to tell me to go to the principal's office.

I skipped to the principal's office. We greeted each other upon my arrival. I sat down across from him. He had my full attention when he informed me, he needed to show me something. He turned on the television. The news was on and me, Cameron, William, and Tonys picture were added to Americas Most Wanted list. I looked down in denial.

Principal Jenkins had a general idea what happened, I didn't add anything. What happened was in the past and I was trying to move forward. I walked to the mini fridge and grabbed us a couple beers. I then sat on the edge of his desk and faced him. He asked if my parents knew, I wasn't sure. We then discussed what to do with his car. We were going to burn it, then drown it in a lake.

I walked to the door, turned around and told principal Jenkins from that day forward he worked for me. He had no issue with it which I didn't expect him to. I left his office and joined my brother and his friends in front of the school. Our parents picked us up and took us home. I went to Cameron's room when inside and our parents went to the attic. Me and Cam looked at each other and thought it was strange our parents were going in the attic. They usually didn't go up there for anything.

I asked Cameron what his homework assignments were so I could do them for him. He couldn't tell me for the life of him what his assignments were, that irritated me. If I was making sure his work was getting done most of the time, the least he could do was help me. I pulled my cellphone out and called one of his classmates. A girl named Susan informed me of everything, which was quite a bit to do for one assignment. I did his homework as fast as I could, but it still took me a little over three hours. Since I didn't have any homework, we chatted for a bit while we played a zombie game on his Xbox.

Just when we thought our parents didn't know the crimes we committed, they stormed into Cameron's room and turned off our video game. They stood in front of the television so we couldn't turn it back on. They demanded an explanation for the news story. We told them we were in a bit of a jam, but it was under control. Our parents proceeded to tell us they would help us through anything, no matter what it was. On their way out our mother gave us five hundred dollars each. We hugged and thanked them.

Me and Cam sat down and turned our game on again. Cam three way called Tony and William. We let them know what our plan was regarding principal Jenkins's car. We added that our parents knew what we were up to and if he got caught, they would pay our bond. We all felt relieved, but we had to work twice as hard not to get caught. Cameron hung up the phone and focused more on the game. My mind drifted for a little.

I couldn't believe we were on a path of crime. My fantasies were no longer fantasies. The life I imagined I wanted to live was finally my reality. Honestly, it was a hell of a lot for me to take in. At the time I didn't know how my brother and his friends felt about everything. All I knew was depression was sinking in. We couldn't go back in time and change anything.

We heard strange noises in the attic. Hours passed and our parents were still up there. Me and Cameron turned the game off and went into the hallway. Closer we heard muffled screams. Our curiosity grew as the screams got louder. We heard our parents coming and ran back to Cameron's room and closed the door. We were so scared we both hid in his room.

A game of hide and seek went on for an hour with our parents searching for us. When they were fed up, they screamed for us to come out wherever we were. They stressed if we didn't hurry, we would be in trouble. Cameron came out first and I followed. Our parents wanted us to follow them to the attic. We followed them into the attic. There was a man bound to a chair.

Blood dripped from the man's face. My father told him if he screamed when he removed the tape from his mouth, he would kill him. He removed the tape; the man didn't scream. Instead, he begged for his life. My mother punched him a few times in the face as if he was a punching bag. The brutal attack caused him to swallow four of his teeth. Me and Cameron stood there wondering what the hell our parents wanted with us.

Our father then said to us "don't feel sorry for this man, this man has stolen from us." Our parents couldn't get their money back from the old man. He gambled it all away. We understood the rage our parents had against the man, but whatever they were going to do to him we didn't want any part of it. I tried to run but I couldn't get out of there. It was extremely hot up there. I hated the fact our parents chose the attic for what they called "playtime.'

Both our parents explained why they brought us up there. They wanted us to join a dangerous cult they were leaders of. They would hire us as contract killers, and we would work for them a lifetime. When I heard lifetime, I cut them off and asked for elaboration. Our mother then left the attic for a few minutes. She returned with two certificates. The certificates were death certificates.

They forced us to sign the certificate, they told us if we ever broke our promise to be a part of the cult until death do us part, they would murder us. Cameron and I stood there not wanting to work for our parents. We wanted to do our own thing. It was a big issue, but I had to admit the money our parents told us we would make made it extremely difficult not to accept the offer. They told us what our first mission was. It was to kill the man in front of us. Mother handed Cameron an aluminum baseball bat.

He was too scared to kill the man that he gave the bat to me. I walked closer to the man. My mother stood so close to me I felt her breath on the back of my neck. I held the bat in the air and looked the man in his eyes. He was indeed fearful for his life, which was understandable. I closed my eyes and hit him as many times as I could. I didn't open my eyes until he was dead.

My mother set the camera to take a group picture with the dead man in the photo. My father stood behind the man and placed his hands on the side of his lips and pushed upward into a smile so he could smile with the rest of us in the picture. Our parents officially lost their minds in our eyes, and they didn't give a damn about our emotions. The man was left in the attic for a few hours. We went to the family room and me and Cameron sat on the sofas. When our parents left the room, we whispered for a little. We hadn't processed our bullshit or theirs.

Our parents returned to the family room with one bag full of money. Since Cameron was too afraid to kill the man, he wasn't rewarded. I opened the bag and saw stacks and stacks of cash rubber band. My father wanted me to follow him into a room he called money machine. He had a giant money counting machine. It was beautiful. I placed the money in the machine, and it counted it, I got eighty-grand that night.

Chapter 3

Our parents went to bed while me and Cameron got rid of the man's body in the attic. We went to the basement and chopped up his body. We placed different body parts in different bags and scattered his body parts in different areas of Texas. Afterwards we went to William's house. I met his grandpa. I found out he talked a lot. He stopped us before we could go to Williams room and talked to us for thirty minutes.

William had to come get me and Cameron for his grandpa to end his conversation with us. When we got to Williams room, we played the new Grand Theft Auto game that he got at the time which was the fifth one. We played it for hours and drank a few beers. I drove my parents Bentley that night and I didn't want me or my brother to crash it, but we had to get home. Just as we were leaving Williams house our mother called us. Cameron answered his cellphone. She wanted to know if we had taken care of the body that was in the attic.

I answered our mother's question and told her we were on the way home. We stopped at a gas station and got gas. We made it home thirty minutes later. We were happy we made it home safely, we almost died twice during the drive home. It was dark in every room when we got in the house. We were so drunk we couldn't find a light to turn on to save our lives. We held hands until we made it upstairs.

We went to our rooms and went straight to bed. The next morning, I drove our parents Ferrari to school. On our way we stopped and picked up Tony and William. William reeked of alcohol, he stumbled to the car. Me and Cameron got out and helped him inside. We buckled him in, then ourselves. Principle Jenkins met us in the parking lot.

We trailed him to the lake we planned to drown the car. We set the car on fire to get rid of the evidence. We watched the car burn until the fire ceased, we then put the car into the lake and watched it go under. Principal Jenkins was concerned about the trouble we were in. Cameron told him our parents had our backs if we ever ran into any trouble. He made sure we heard him loud and clear as well. He wanted us to know we could call him for anything.

Our principal drove us back to school. Cameron, William, and Tony went to their classes went to my third period; my teacher wasn't there. For whatever reason we waited for her to show but she never did. As we were leaving our teacher appeared. The lesson for that day was very short. In fact, it was so short as soon as I sat down class was dismissed.

Everyone was extremely pissed. On our way out we figured out a way we could get revenge. I waited until every student left the class to make a move. When the class was empty, me and a couple others snuck inside. We destroyed everything of value. When our teacher returned, she had no idea she was filmed. She found out shortly after her daughter watched it.

My third period classroom was destroyed, literally, from the ceiling to the floor. An investigation was made and ironically our teacher was the one found guilty. Charges were placed against her, she had to serve two years. After she served her time, she went after my other two classmates and killed them. She almost shot me in my sleep. My alarm saved my life. When it went off and I reached for it, it fell.

I went to the cafeteria and stood in line for lunch. I saw William and Tony and a girl hanging with them. My brother was behind them with a new girl on his arm. She was a transfer student from California. My brother was promiscuous. He had so many girlfriends that I found it extremely difficult to remember their names most of the time. His girl turned around and attempted to initiate a conversation with me, but I wasn't focused on her, I wanted to know who the girl was with William and Tony.

I skipped the line until I stood by William and Tony. The girl with them was fifteen-year-old Lily Shaw. She was Tonys sister, they looked nothing alike. Lily and I chatted for a while and ate lunch together. The guys ate separately at another table. I found Lily to be a cool chick once I got a chance to know her. I liked the fact she was an easy person to talk to.

Lily was just as money hungry as the rest of us, but greed was what had us in the predicament we were in. We couldn't turn back the hands of time. If me and the guys were to start our own crew, we would need another girl. So many thoughts circled my brain, she was perfect for the crew. My plan was to compose a blood ritual that night to sacrifice our lives. Death do us part as I thought it would be another death certificate. The only difference would be it would be served by me instead of my parents.

After school when our parents picked us up, we were followed by Arlington police. After my father sped up, they turned their sirens on. We were arrested and taken downtown for questioning. We had nothing to fear, our parents took care of everything. They rescued us so fast it seemed as though we left as soon as we got there. Our parents took us out for dinner to a Chinese buffet. We stuffed our mouths until we could no longer eat.

Me and Cameron went to our rooms as soon as we were home. I began to take a shower and we heard our parents on the intercom. I turned off the water and listened.

They told us we weren't going to school the next day; they had some people we needed to meet. I was happy we didn't have to go to school the next day but at the same time I was anxious to know what the day would bring. Tony and William were in Cameron's room when I got out the shower. I got dressed and joined them down the hall.

I cancelled the ritual that night since Lily couldn't make it. The guys followed me down the hall to the game room. Before we played anything me and Cam discussed with William and Tony what our parents forced us to do the night before. Their response irritated us; they saw nothing wrong with what our parents did to us. They felt we were lucky to have an opportunity to kill people for a living and get paid for it. Me and Cameron dropped the subject. There was no point continuing it.

Our issue was we didn't want to be forced to do anything. If we had to wake up every day and risk our lives, we wanted full control. We played race car games so long we passed out where we played. The next morning, me and Cameron woke up early and forced Tony and William out. Me and Cameron thought we could get a little more sleep, but our parents went to the kitchen and banged on pots and pans to wake us. We had ten minutes to get ready. We went downstairs forty-five minutes later.

Our parents were angry with us, which we expected them to be. On our way to the abandoned warehouse our parents did most of their kills at they told us our first lesson for the day was obedience. They told us if we couldn't obey orders, we would have messy kills. If we left behind evidence that was an example of a messy kill. We got to the warehouse an hour later. We pulled up to a tall white gate. A few seconds later the gate opened.

Dad drove the trail, a mile later he parked in front of the warehouse. This was the biggest warehouse we'd ever seen. Two white men with silver hair stood on each side of the front door with Ak-47 rifles. We got out the car and approached the men. Both men greeted our parents, then our parents introduced us as their children. The men were thrilled when they heard of two high schoolers working for their parents as contract killers. Me and Cameron looked at each other, then starred at the men until the doors were closed behind us.

We followed our parents to an elevator and went to the fourth floor. There were so many people on the fourth floor. I wondered how many were on the other floors. Our parents took us to a private room where there was a man who appeared as a surgeon. There was a woman who was dead on an operating table. Her chest had been ripped open. I was disgusted by the level of brutality, but I was also intrigued.

Our parents left us alone with the strange man. We found out the man was a surgeon, he worked closely with my father at the hospital not far from our house. The man sat down and introduced himself as Dr. Ping. His last name tickled us, but we tried to hide it. However, we were given the green light to laugh. He explained he was named after his father and why. His father died a few years ago as the world's best ping pong player. Although we weren't interested in the game it wasn't often, we heard stories with purpose.

Me and Cameron walked closer to the woman's body that was on his table. We leaned over and looked inside her chest. Where her heart should've been, it was no longer there. During their five-year relationship he couldn't trust her. She cheated with multiple men and multiple women. Ironically, he cheated on her as well. He was married, but it ended when she found out about the affair.

Dr. Ping placed the corpse in a freezer and locked it. He took us to every floor and introduced us as our parents

James and Jenny's children. He did this so everyone would know we weren't the ones to fuck with. We walked and talked with him. On our way to a room called the theater he taught lesson number two which was "never work with someone we can't trust." When inside the theater he shared lesson number three which was to always pay attention to our surroundings. He left us to watch a movie.

The movie ended, we walked around unsupervised for an hour. Within that time, we saw all types of weird shit. We saw orgies, drugs, dead bodies, and a hell of a lot of money. Although we didn't want to be there, maybe our friends were right, maybe we needed to ease up on our parents and enjoy ourselves. We locked ourselves in a room filled with money. We played in it until our parents found us. They stood firm with no expression on their faces.

Cameron was caught on a video call with William and Tony. He ended it when he realized our parents were behind him. Our mother took his phone and called them back. We thought he was in trouble, but he wasn't. She simply told them the visual of the money would've lasted longer if they were there with us. Cameron laughed when he took his phone. Our parents then left us to enjoy the room for another ten minutes.

The ride home was rather annoying. Our parents kept quizzing us on everything we learned at the warehouse. Although Cameron and I answered all their questions correctly, that didn't matter. Once we were home, we were happy to have some time away from them for a while. I rolled two joints in my room shortly after we got there. We each took one and lit it. We coughed so much our eyes were red and tears rolled down our cheeks.

A couple hours passed, and we were still chocking on the marijuana. Our parents entered and waited for us to get ourselves together. It amazed me that both myself and brother were on the floor and neither one of them helped us. Their actions disturbed my spirit so much that even after I was okay, I purposely laid on the floor a bit longer. The look in my mothers' eyes was a look we rarely saw. I knew she was livid, but I still didn't move. My brother didn't have my back, he stood up to them and apologized.

I was sick to my stomach watching him grovel to them for forgiveness. Thirty minutes passed and I still hadn't moved. I was just as stubborn as my mother was. My brother pulled me up. When I looked up, I was eye to eye with her. I stared into her dreamy light brown eyes and still didn't apologize. My father reached into his left jean pocket and pulled out a copy of our death certificates.

I followed my father into the living room area. I sat on the couch, and he left for a few minutes. I looked around as if I was a visitor in a stranger's home. My father came back with a large garbage bag filled with something. I stood up wondering what the hell he was doing. He placed his hand into the bag and pulled out one of my video games. He then bent down and leaned towards the fireplace.

That was enough to send me over the edge. I ran towards my father and begged him not to drop it in the fire. I found myself in the same situation as my brother was not long ago. The only difference is he found his head and I lost mine. I looked at my father with tears in my eyes. I apologized but it was too late. He dropped it in the fire and said to me if I ever disrespected him or my mother again, he would destroy all my games.

I walked away from my father with rage boiling inside. I joined mom and Cameron in my room again. I flopped down onto my bed and pulled out my cellphone. I went to Amazon and checked the item to see if they had any more in stock. My father reentered my room and explained why he and my mother were in there to begin with. I listened and glanced at my phone. My number one video game wasn't in stock.

Our parents informed us of another bounty. There was a bounty of five hundred-thousand-dollars placed on the head of an elderly woman. Our parents wanted her son, but his mother went through great lengths to protect him as any mother who loved their child/children would. They wanted the closest person to him. His mother was his best friend. They had lunch together every day for 10 years. That changed when his mother feared for his life.

The next day at school my three enemies bullied me all day. They usually bullied me every day. I fought all three of them a few times in the past, but I always lost. They jumped me every day and every day I had to explain the bruises to my parents. Tired was an understatement. I was mentally, emotionally, physically, and spiritually drained. However, I continued taking the blows every day, at the right time I would have my revenge.

Later that day I met my brother in the stairwell to smoke a blunt, well so I thought. Just as I was to light it, he stopped me. He pulled out a mini Ziplock bag that contained a white substance. He dangled it in my face. I starred at the substance and thought of what it could've been. He asked me if I knew what it was, I guessed Cocaine. I guessed right he said.

Cameron opened the bag, placed a finger inside and licked it. I tried to take the bag from him, I didn't want him doing at all. We wrestled for a few minutes, eventually I got the bag from him. I ran to the trash can, but I didn't make it. He tripped me and snatched it back. The second time around I witnessed him snort it. It broke my heart to see him in that light.

I ran to principal Jenkins's office not knowing my brother was behind me. I snatched the bag and threw it on our principal's desk. I wanted him to talk to my brother in hopes he would take it seriously. Instead, principal Jenkins had some of his own and threw his on his desk. My brother took his bag and put it in his backpack. He dared me to do some. It was a bet I took, if I hadn't, he wouldn't have let it go.

Principal Jenkins pulled out his wallet and removed a credit card. He then opened his bag of blow and poured a little onto one of the corners of the card. He handed it to me, I lost a little from my hands shaking. Ten minutes passed and the card was finally close enough to my nose to do the deed. My brother cheered me on, I closed my eyes and snorted it. My right nostril went numb.

I lit a cigarette to perfect my high. Strangely I liked it, it scared me how much I liked it. My brother and our principal did a few lines over the course of thirty minutes. I was so high my thoughts were racing faster than my heart. I had to admit over a game of pool in the office that was some good shit. My brother smiled at me and told me if I ever wanted to try it again his connect could hook us up with the purest quality. I smiled at him not because I wanted more but because I couldn't feel my face.

After school Julie, Jessica, and Jennifer waited for me and my brother outside. Our parents had not showed up yet. Jennifer, the leader of her sisters took my backpack and tore up everything I had inside. Everything was ruined, especially two homework assignments I wouldn't be able to turn in. My brother retrieved what he could, but it wasn't enough to put anything back together. The girls turned their backs towards us when their parents arrived in front of the school.

I gave everyone a show they didn't want to miss. I pulled Jennifer's ponytail. She fell back into my breasts. Surprisingly her sisters didn't come to her rescue. They yelled for her from the backseat of their dad's truck. Jennifer weighed less than I did, without her sisters running to her aid she struggled. She wanted me off her, but I wouldn't let go of her hair or her throat. She bit my arm so hard I had to let her go.

Jennifer fell to the ground holding her throat. Her sisters and father continued yelling at her to hurry up. I stood over her and looked down. I wanted to kick her in her face, but the sound of my father's horn stopped me. My brother literally followed in my footsteps. We both walked on Jennifer's body to get to our fathers Benz. When inside Jennifer's father ran to her, picked her up, put her into the passenger seat, and buckled her in.

Chapter 4

Our father got angry when he found out what happened between me and Jennifer. Jennifer's father had not pulled off the school parking lot yet. Our father pulled up beside him and honked his horn. When he had Mr. Johnsons attention, he threatened him. He told him if any one of his girls destroy my homework again, he would kill his girls first so he would have to watch, then kill him and his wife. Mr. Johnson was more bark than bite. He had no idea our father was serious as a heart-attack.

Our father sped off angrily, me and Cameron feared for our lives. That was the longest fifteen-minute ride home we ever had. Shortly after he parked in the garage, we got out the car and ran into the house before he could say anything to us. We thought Friday would be our typical relaxed start of the weekend like it normally was, but our father had other plans for us. Our mother still hadn't come home yet, and I wondered if our father acting strange had anything to do with her absence. Me and Cameron had ten minutes to change our clothes. The dress code was all black, I hated that, ironically, I felt I got dressed for a funeral.

We met our father downstairs in the kitchen. Cameron sat on one of the stools at the counter, I pulled a chair out from the dinner table and sat down. Our father James said to us "as a family we must represent the family last name, failure to do so will result in a death." Neither my brother nor I responded to his statement. We stared blankly into our father's eyes. He continued to explain what it meant to be a Johnson. We didn't give a shit about the family name.

Shit was out of control, but I remembered this was exactly what I wished for the first day of our junior year of high school. At that moment when I realized what I wished for while our father continued the subject of upholding the family last name, I wished I hadn't made that wish. Our father excited the kitchen when he finished talking. He wanted us to find the keys to his chevy that was parked alongside the Benz in the garage. Our parents owned a few cars. My favorite was the Porsche. I loved how low the car sat, I always felt like I was a race car driver every time I drove it.

We searched the house for the Chevys car keys. Cameron found them. On our way out the house our father handed us both a red ski mask. I didn't understand why we had to wear all black if his intentions were to give us a red ski mask. Cameron placed his mask over his head and looked at me. I ran to the chevy when our father unlocked it. I was the first inside followed by Cameron then James.

The garage door opened, our father pulled out his check book and made two checks out to us. He handed them to us then drove forward and pressed the garage button to close it. For whatever reason I was overwhelmed about everything, I didn't look at the amount on the it. My brother looked at his check then showed me. My eyes got big as hell, our parents were paying us more and more. Our father drove us to a park thirty minutes outside of Arlington. He backed into a parking space and turned the car off.

James exited the vehicle and proceeded towards the trail. We assumed he wanted us to follow him, but we waited five minutes to join him. Cameron pulled out the cocaine and sniffed a line, I did the same. I needed something to calm my nerves, but it only made me more anxious to do whatever our father needed us to do. Cameron did a second line and so did I. Our father had no idea we had been dabbling into drugs and I wanted to keep it that way. We got the car and locked it.

A half of mile on the trail we found our father. He asked why we looked strange, we looked up at him and acted like we didn't understand what he was referring to. He dropped the matter and informed us on why he drove us to the park. He told us for this hit we had to do a hell of a lot of running. I looked at James as if he was a stranger. I wasn't fond of running, my chubby ass wouldn't make it long. He made us run ten laps.

Although I didn't want to run the laps, the coke, like before gave me a boost. It was hilarious to me that I was bigger than my brother and I finished my laps first. I was exhausted as hell afterwards. I thought I was gone die. It took me twenty minutes to catch my breath. By the time I caught my breath Cameron finished his laps. He was just as exhausted as I was.

I walked to the chevy and leaned back on the hood. My father honked his horn for me to get off. I didn't move immediately. He continued honking until I moved. I was so tired, my father had to get out the car, put me over his shoulder, and put me in the passenger seat. He closed the door and I buckled myself in. I looked up and saw Cameron on the ground.

He appeared dead but we knew he wasn't. James got out the car and walked towards Cameron. He poured water on his face. Cameron awoke angrily, he put his hands up to block the water. His attempt to block the water didn't stop our father. Cameron tugged on our father's pants to help him get up. Cameron stood up and walked slowly to the car.

I got in the backseat and laid across it. I closed my eyes, I wanted to escape in my dreams, but I didn't have the opportunity to do so. James wanted me to drive. I hopped in the driver seat while my father slid to the passenger and Cameron to the backseat. An address was given to me shortly after I started the car. Our father explained who we had to execute and why. A young stripper in her twenties was hired by our father one night to perform for his friends.

Upon her arrival she was taken to a room to change into her outfit. She never changed into her outfit, in fact she never had intentions to dance. An hour passed and she still hadn't joined the men. Our father went to check on her and she was nowhere to be found. After searching the room our father left her in, she stole the money he intended to give her if she performed well. She stole over fifty-grand. She could've gotten that plus more had she followed through with her promise, but she chose to fuck our father over and neither one of our parents would allow that bullshit to slide.

We arrived at the girl's mother's mansion. Her mother was wealthy, she had the type of money that made itself. The mansion was by far the largest mansion we'd ever seen, our mansion was a little smaller. However, I was certain if our parents wanted a bigger house, they most definitely could've afforded it. I parked the Chevy down the block. The woman's house was so huge it was as if we parked in the driveway. The house and driveway took up half the block.

Me and Cameron put our ski masks on and got out the car. We walked halfway down the block and approached a gate. The gate was too small for the mansion. We easily jumped over it. The driveway went on for miles. It took us fifteen minutes to make it to the house. I felt I couldn't go any further, I was out of breath and so was Cameron.

We hid in their cornfield located in the back of the house. My brothers phone rang a few times, but he ignored the calls. He was too tired to reach in his pocket and pull it out to answer it. I took my backpack off and opened it. I took out two bottles of water for us then my cellphone rang. I thought of not answering but I was curious to find out who it was. It wouldn't have been our father, he told us everything we needed to know prior to our arrival.

I answered the call, our mother was outraged Cameron ignored her calls. Although she wanted an explanation, she didn't press the issue. We didn't have much time to execute our mission. Our mother was there to help us get into the house as easily as possible. We needed help but our father was strict about executing the mission ourselves. I strongly felt me, and Cameron could handle it. I thanked our mother for her time, me and Cameron had it from there.

I located the power box near the basement back door, I switched the lights off. Our mother left us and joined our father in the car. Meanwhile, I picked the lock to the basement back door and we snuck in. When inside we couldn't see anything. Cameron tripped over a bucket of paint and fell into a wall causing everything to fall off the shelves. I found him in the darkness and helped him up. We stood still for a moment, scared the noise alerted the girl and her mother.

We ran up a few steps and found the door leading out the basement. I picked the lock and entered their kitchen. My plan worked to perfection. I knew when I switched their lights off it would lead them outside, during that time my plan was to sneak inside before they returned. Cameron sat on the kitchen counter. I opened the refrigerator and pulled out hamburger meat. I worked myself around the kitchen and grabbed everything I needed to prepare cheeseburgers.

Anita the stripper and her mother walked into their house confused. By this time their lights were switched back on. They heard us in the kitchen. Vicky, Anita's mother, tried to run upstairs to her room and get her gun, but I stopped her. Somehow, I knew it would be one of their moves. Vicky walked down the stairs, together her and her daughter joined us in the kitchen. They were shaken with fear, they stood there and watched me cook.

I served myself and my brother. I sat down at the table and introduced myself then informed them of the reason of our visit. When we finished eating, I grabbed our plates and threw them into the sink. I looked at Anita and pointed to the dishes. She starred at me and didn't move. I walked over to where she sat and kneeled. I told her if she didn't wash those dishes, I would break every one of them and use every piece to cut her with.

Anita ran to the sink and washed the dishes. When she finished, we all went into the living room and sat on the two couches. They pleaded with us not to kill them. I requested the money from Anita, but she didn't have it. I went into the kitchen and grabbed the biggest butcher's knife. I returned to the living room. I stood in the doorway scratching my head with the knife.

I asked Anita if she wanted to live, she cried and screamed "yes." I shifted my attention to her mother. I stated to her if she couldn't help her daughter, she would have a funeral to prepare for. Anita's mother Joyce ran upstairs and brought down a checkbook with her. I looked at my brother and smiled. She made the check out to me. She paid the amount our father was owed.

I took the check and placed it in my wallet. On our way out my brother took my gun and shot them both between the eyes. I was a bit irritated with him, he didn't have to do that since they cooperated. He took our fathers words literally, but I couldn't get mad at him for following orders. I called our dad and told him to meet us at the stop sign at the end of the street. We ran down the driveway and hopped over the gate into the street. We were tired and hoped our parents had seen us.

Our mom spotted us and stopped the car in the middle of the street. We got in and our mom sped off. Our parents were extremely proud of us for executing the mission by ourselves. That's all they talked about until we arrived home. Our father had a surprise for us, we followed him for a few minutes. We reached a gold giant door, it appeared to be a volt. Our dad opened it and it was empty, my heart was crushed.

Although the volt was empty it was still exciting to have it. We could store all our money in there from each hit. The thought of that excited me as well. Me and Cameron thought our day was over, but our mom had one last gift for us. We met her in the garage. There was a car that was covered with a sheet. Cameron pulled the sheet off and we saw the candy red Bentley.

Our mother gave me the keys. We didn't have our driver's license but that didn't stop us from taking the car. We test drove it at eleven o clock that night. We weren't a block away from the house when a cop behind us turned his siren on. Cameron panicked, he had drugs on him. I told him to remain calm, it wasn't an issue until it was an issue. I slowed down and pulled over.

I turned the car off and kept both hands on the steering wheel. The officer approached us, he wanted us out the car. We were both stubborn as hell, we didn't flinch an inch on his first demand. The officer attitude went from zero to a hundred quickly. He busted out my window and tugged on my left arm for us to exit the vehicle. Cameron got out, slammed the car door, flopped himself on the hood of the car, and put his hands behind his back. The officer cuffed him.

The officer walked my brother to his vehicle, opened the door, and shoved him into the backseat. His attention was then shifted back to me. I thought he broke my arm; I could no longer feel it. He walked slowly towards my direction; I exited the Bentley as slowly as he walked. I did exactly what my brother did. I flopped on the hood of the car and put both hands behind my back. The officer pulled me off the hood and wacked me a few times in my stomach with his baton.

I got a good look at the officer's name before he shoved me into the backseat alongside my brother. He shoved me so hard that my head had fallen into Cameron's lap. I picked my head up and looked at Officer Wicks. He punched me as hard as he could in my left eye then slammed the door. My cellphone rang as the officer sped off. He stopped in the middle of the street, got out, came into the backseat, and took both our phones. He dropped both phones in the street and crushed them.

My stomach felt worse than my busted eye did, I cried in my brother's lap. The officer drove us to an unknown location and threw us out the car like we were trash. We were still in cuffs, and we had miles and miles to walk back to where the Bentley was left. Six hours passed and we finally made it back to the car. My brother drove us home, he carried me in the house and laid me on the couch. He took the elevator to our father's library, luckily, he was still awake. Cameron explained everything that happened.

Our father rushed to my aid. He lifted my shirt and saw the bruises on my stomach. Cameron made the lights brighter; our father had seen my eye. He thought it was best we didn't disturb our mother with it. He asked me a few questions. I answered them to the best of my ability. After he treated my wounds and my eye, I told him the officer's name.

Our father told us not to worry about anything. He would find the officer for us, and we would have the pleasure of executing his bitch ass. I was in no condition to go to school. I stayed home a few days so my eye could heal.

When I returned to school a meeting was held in the gymnasium. Me and my brother joined the other students and staff members. A twelve-year-old boy who was a genius was found dead under the bleachers of the track field.

Everyone was shocked, especially me and Cameron. We had to find our who else amongst us was a murderer. We waved at principal Jenkins when we saw him. There was a man who stood next to him who looked exactly like the man that arrested us a few nights ago. We could only see the right side of his face. I starred at the man until we had a full visual. Principal Jenkins dismissed everyone an hour later, me and Cameron stayed seated.

We were the last students in the gymnasium. We had a full visual of the officer, the man was indeed Officer Wicks. When he walked out, me and Cameron ran down the bleachers and chatted with our principal. We found out everything we needed to know. He had a twin brother, wife, and three young boys. All we needed was his address. Principal Jenkins would give it to us when the school day ended.

Me and Cameron bumped into Tony and William in the hallway. Tony's sister lily joined us shortly after. Cameron had given them an update of everything that happened to us during the time we were apart. Lily stated our story was like a horror movie. I looked at her and said, "our story is like a horror movie because this world is evil". We all departed ways and went to class. My third and fourth period teachers had been fired, they both threatened a few students.

I couldn't blame the teachers for having to use excess force with the students. Most of the students were bad as hell, often teachers gave up because they usually had difficulty reaching the students, they wouldn't listen. My third period teacher was replaced by a man named Rocky

Hats. I laughed hard as hell with my classmates. We thought the man was joking but he was serious. Our new teacher was a total geek, and his voice was scratchy. He wrote our homework assignment on the board and began the lesson for the day.

I closed my eyes and apologized to the creator, I opened my eyes and thought to myself Mr. Hats was by far the ugliest man I ever met. I had met some ugly people, but he was at the top of my list. Two girls who sat close to me chatted as if they bumped their heads. They were attracted to that weirdo. I was appalled, I starred at them until class was dismissed. I was so appalled I followed the girls to their next class; I had no idea I was in the wrong class until the teacher called roll and I wasn't on her list. When I stood up to leave it was the first time I blinked since I heard the girl's comment.

I went to my fourth period class and was greeted by a woman whose hairline was pushed so far back no one in my class, including myself could take her seriously. I laughed so hard the wounds on my abdomen hurt badly. She taught the class as best as she could. I could tell she was embarrassed but it took courage for her to come to school like that. She paired us in groups of two. We had a report to do and very little time to do it in. I was paid with Jennifer, my heart dropped.

Chapter 5

I knew if I wanted an A on the report, I had to do it myself. Class was dismissed, I grabbed my backpack and ran far away from Jennifer as I possibly could. I had no idea she followed me to my fifth period. Mr. Jones met her at the door and turned her around. Mr. Jones closed the door and walked to the front of the class. When he started to speak, a student knocked on the door. Since she was late to his class, he ignored her.

Mr. Jones proceeded with the lesson for the day. Ten minutes later every student was asleep including myself. Out of all the students as usual I was the only one awakened. The issue didn't bother me usually, but it did that day. I simply didn't want to be awakened. My schedule outside of school was a strict one and I barely got any sleep. Everything at that moment weighed me down.

What weighed me down mostly at that moment was the thought of Jennifer taking full credit for a report she didn't do. I couldn't allow that to happen, and I wouldn't. Mr. Jones asked me quite a few questions. I knew the answers, but my mind was elsewhere. I failed to answer every question. I stared into his big brown dreamy eyes. I was overwhelmed with anger. He waited for me to answer him, but I never did.

He sent me to principal Jenkins. I happily arose from my seat and skipped to his office. On my way there Jennifer stopped me. As a desperate attempt to escape I lied as a decoy, I told her Justin Timberlake was behind her and her dumb ass fell for it. I ran straight to the principal's office.

The door was locked, it usually was open. I knocked and knocked; he opened the door eventually.

I walked into his office and went straight for the fridge. I grabbed a beer and closed the door. I looked at principal Jenkins and he didn't look well. There were a few lines of coke on his desk. I could tell he had been snorting lines all day. I sipped my beer and he dropped to the floor. I dropped the beer and ran to him.

I shook him and called his name repeatedly. There was no response. I checked him for a pulse, he had one. I needed my brother, I found my cellphone and called him, he didn't answer. I called him a second time while I got rid of the dope. I went into the bathroom he had in his office and poured it down the toilet. I called my brother a third time and flushed the toilet.

My brother finally answered, I was irritated. I didn't have to explain anything, he heard the strain in my voice and came running. There was a knock at the door not long after the call ended. I thought it was Cameron but when I answered it was William, Tony, and Lily. I peeped out and didn't see him. They told me he sent them; he was stuck in class due to a quiz he didn't study for. I had to rescue him, I had to figure something out.

We had to take principal Jenkins to a hospital, we had to find a way to get him out the building without incident. I could see the car from his window. I took my keys out my backpack and pointed them towards the car and unlocked it. We sat him up in his chair and put his arms in his jacket and placed a pair of shades on his face. We stood him up, but he was too heavy to carry. We searched for something we could roll him to the car in. I remembered in the bathroom there was a bucket with a mop in it, I ran into the bathroom and threw the mop out.

I rolled the bucket to where our principal sat. Me and Lily grabbed his arms while Tony and William each took a leg. We managed to slightly move him. He was a big man, and it was ironic because coke to my knowledge was supposed to suppress the appetite. Although we suffered tremendously from his weight, we possessed enough strength to move him to the bucket. We rolled him to the door, and I reached over him to open it. When I turned the knob there was another knock at the door.

William rolled principal Jenkins into the bathroom and closed the door. I was scared to open the door, but I had no choice. Before I opened the door, I whispered for everyone to hid. I closed my eyes and opened it. It was my teacher Mr. Jones. He wanted to speak with principal Jenkins regarding the many of times he had to send me to his office. My heartbeat had increased due to his suspicion of why I was in the office by myself.

I began to sweat, and my voice was shaken. Mr. Jones demanded that I told him the truth, I wondered if I would be punished if I had of. I looked at Mr. Jones with tears in my eyes, I told him principal Jenkins went home for the day and instead of me going back to his class, I decided to stay in the office by myself. Surprisingly he believed me, he hugged me and took me back to his class. I was pissed, William, Tony, and Lily needed my help. Halfway to his class I told him I left something in the principal's office, He looked at me and said "backpack", I looked over my right shoulder, I could see my backpack was not on my back.

My teacher allowed me to go back to the principal's office to get my backpack. He wanted to follow me, but I assured him I would return to his class to get my homework assignment. I ran until I made it to the office. My brother opened the door, I was happy to see him. No longer did we have to rescue him. I looked around the office. I looked through principals Jenkins's belongings, I didn't know exactly what I was looking for, all I knew was he needed a better disguise.

I found a wig in his briefcase, it belonged to one of the many women our principal usually partied with. I placed the blond wig over his head, we were ready to roll him to the car. I opened the door and looked both ways, the halls were clear. I took his car keys and ran to the back door of the school. I pulled his car around and they rolled him to the parking lot and put him in the backseat. Our original plan was to take him to the hospital ourselves, but I figured his wife should've made that decision. Instead, I drove to his house, prior to our arrival I informed her of everything.

Principal Jenkins wife once again met us in the driveway. She screamed when she saw the way he appeared. We helped her get him into her truck. The bucket he was placed in, she disposed of it. We all got in her truck, and she drove us back to school. I had no intentions of collecting the homework from Mr. Jones, I could get the assignment from a classmate. I ran back in the school and locked principal Jenkins's office.

When I turned around my teacher scared the shit out of my ass. It was the first time he creeped me out on another level. The way he stood in front of me inhaling and exhaling the bologna he had for lunch disturbed my spirit. I felt like I was in a dark alley and well you guys know the rest. His breath was by far the worst I ever smelt, I wanted to vomit. He handed me my assignment and I ran to the front of the school and got in the car. Cameron sped off the parking lot and drove to William's house.

We went inside and there his grandpa was naked on the couch and covered in feces. William awakened him and helped him to the shower. The rest of closed our eyes and ran out the house. William didn't want to be left alone but to

44

us that was more than we could handle. I drove Tony and his sister Lily to their grandparents' home. I parked on the street. Me and Cameron followed them inside and we met their mother along with their grandparents.

Their mother kept dozing off after every word she spoke. Tony and Lily tried to shift our attention by taking us in the back to Tonys room, but their grandparents were against it. Their mother was a heroin addict. She desperately wanted full custody of her children, but her parents were totally against it which was understandable. I asked where the bathroom was, I was pointed in the direction. I thought I would have a moment to be alone, but Tony and Lily's grandmother walked with me to the bathroom. I closed the door, sat on the toilet, and looked down.

The woman paced back and forth in front of the bathroom door. I messaged my brother, and he watched her watch that door. We were treated like criminals in the household. Although me and my brother were criminals and everyone in town knew our faces, we had power. With power we felt invincible. A few minutes later I whipped my ass and flushed the toilet. I walked to the sink to wash my hands but there was no soap.

I looked in the cabinet under the sink for soap. There was one bar, I reached in toward the back and grabbed it. Behind the soap was a jar full of condoms. I was stunned. Tony and Lily's grandparents were strict, I wondered which one of them smuggled them in and why they did. I turned on the faucet and washed my hands. I unlocked the bathroom door and opened the door.

Their grandmother was still there. I rushed past her and looked at my brother. I pointed at the front door; my brother's reaction was the fastest I'd ever seen. He bypassed me and almost knocked me down. He was already in the car. I wanted to join him, but Lily got my attention. I joined her in what I thought was her bedroom, it wasn't long after I found out her and tony shared a room.

I stood there and starred at her as she spoke. I didn't hear anything she said to me. It dawned on me the condoms in the bathroom were Tony's. I hoped to God they weren't sexually involved. The more I tried to shift my thoughts, the more I realized what usually went on in that bedroom. Lily wasn't finished talking but I had to get out that house. I didn't want to assume anything, but it was hard not to, it was directly in my face.

Once again, I ran out the house to the car. When my brother saw me, he moved to the passenger seat. I was still stunned. I didn't know exactly how I would tell him about his friends. Despite my fears, I took a deep breath and told him my thoughts. He had no response at first, he was as stunned as I was, but he had known them for years and it was difficult for him to accept that. He told me their grandparents were strange individuals, but there was no way his friends could and would be sexually involved due to the strict rules of the household.

I asked Cameron if he thought it was abnormal for Lily and Tony to share a bedroom, especially at their ages. His response informed me he was still oblivious to everything. It stunned me more he had been their friend for a few years, and he never noticed. Something as big as that doesn't surface overnight. Perhaps it was the reason their grandparents were strict, and perhaps something sinister was going on. I started the car, my brother stated he was hungry. I drove to one of my favorite restaurants.

We arrived at Cut & Bourbon; we hadn't been in years. When inside there was a long wait time. I was determined to get a table. I walked into the kitchen and asked for the manager. The chefs wanted me out the kitchen, but I wasn't leaving until I spoke with the manager. I didn't want any trouble. All I wanted was a table and a menu.

Cameron went to the bathroom. Meanwhile, there I stood in the kitchen arguing with the head chef. After a while, I stopped. She continued, when she no longer got a reaction from me, she charged at me. I grabbed a flag that was to the left of me and wrapped her in it. The manager was on his way to the area, as a finishing touch I placed tape around her head to her throat in hopes she would suffocate. The manager waited for me to finish.

I handed the manager a few hundred dollars for a table. He smiled and informed me a table was available. We left the kitchen and walked into the dining hall. I looked around, there was no table available. He walked towards a table where two extremely obese women sat. They had over ten plates on the table. Mr. Williams, the manager, kicked both the women out of the restaurant.

The two women had been there over six hours. During that time, they consumed a great deal of food. Mr. Williams stated to the women he would no longer serve them; they were too greedy. Both women were offended. One of them passed gas before leaving. I was absolutely disgusted; I no longer wanted the booth. The smell was horrendous, so horrendous many people walked out his restaurant.

My brother looked forward to dinner at one of the best spots in town as well as did I, but we were both disappointed that evening. We left and Cameron drove us home. A silver Cadillac was parked in the driveway. We figured it was our grandparents, our grandparents on our father's side. They were the only ones we knew who drove a silver caddy. What was supposed to be a beautiful visit turned into a bad one. All our parents and grandparents did was argue.

John and Jackie, our father's parents, strongly felt me and Cameron were better off with them. We loved them but we didn't have a desire to leave with them. Me and Cameron snuck pass them and went to my room. We discussed the possibility of having to finish our junior and senior year at our grandparents. Neither one of us wanted that as our reality. We loved the city too much to leave, our grandparents lived in the boondocks. Literally the middle of nowhere.

We thought our folks were oblivious to the fact we were home, but they had known we were home from the moment we walked through the door. Our father called my cellphone, I rolled my eyes, and purposely didn't answer. I declined the call and sent him to voicemail. He left a message. I listened to the message; we had no choice but to go downstairs. Cameron took the elevator downstairs and joined them in the kitchen. They waited for me to join them, ten minutes later I was still in my bedroom.

I played a video game to pass time, Cameron followed our grandfather outside. His wife found me, she wanted me to pack all my clothes. She sat beside me on my bed. I took my gaming headphones off; I was forced to listen. She stated our parents weren't good parents. I looked her angrily although she was right. She believed me and Cameron would have a better future if we made the right decision which in her opinion was the best decision.

I ran downstairs into my mother's arms. My mother consoled me. My father walked away, I expected that from him. Rarely did he show his sensitive side. When he did my mother was the only one who he felt he could be vulnerable with. He hated his parents, well at least everyone thought he did. I guess their relationship was more so a tough loved one.

My mother whispered in my ear, "no matter what happens baby girl, your father and I will find you and your brother". My granny pulled me away from my mother, I cried. She took my hand and led me outside to where my brother and grandfather were. Me and Cameron starred at each other while they discussed the living arrangement. I could feel my brother's pain. We both backed up slowly until we were close to the front door. I opened it and we ran inside; I locked our grandparents out.

They ran to the door furious. We found our parents, I asked if they had enough for us for dinner. They had more than enough food prepared we sat down and enjoyed a delightful meal. Our grandparents eventually left. We all high-fived each other when we saw them back out the driveway. It was the first time they sped off that we had seen. Shortly after the house phone rang, a heated message was left for us.

After school the next day we arrived home to find all our belongings packed. My brother and I searched the house for our parents but neither one of them were home. We wanted an explanation. I ran to living room where I left my phone on the couch, my phone was nowhere to be found. I retraced my steps throughout the house although I was certain I left it on the couch. I was agitated and I didn't understand. My brother ran to his room and rolled a couple joints for us.

The bright head lights in the driveway dazzled me and the loud music irritated me furthermore. Our parents arrived. The joints Cameron rolled, I lit them both at the same time. He laughed and snatched one from my mouth. I snatched it back and ran outside. Our mother was teary-eyed and our father distant as usual. We followed them inside.

Our mother had taken the elevator to her private study. My brother and I stood at the bottom of the stairs for a few minutes. Meanwhile, our father went to my bedroom first, a few seconds later he dropped all my luggage's over the railing. Not long after he did the same thing to Cameron. When he finished, he told us what we already knew, we had to move in with our grandparents. We grabbed some of all luggage's and put them into one of the six monster trucks he owned. He made it clear he and our mother couldn't pack everything, we had too much.

They left the rest of our things in our rooms; we could visit anytime. Our father waited for us in the truck. Meanwhile, both my brother and I went to our mother's study. We hugged and kissed her on her cheek. As we were leaving out, she surprised us with a box. One box was given to each of us. Inside the box was every drug that existed.

My brother was ecstatic, on the other hand I was in disbelief. In that moment I realized she didn't give a damn about us. For a mother to destroy her children's life in that way spoke for itself. I had nothing to say, unlike my brother, I couldn't thank her for that. I left their presence and ran downstairs to a bathroom. I kneeled in front of the toilet and cried. I then flushed the drugs down the toilet and disposed of the box.

I could've easily given my share to Cameron, but he didn't need it. he had more than enough. I prayed that I never had to witness him overdosing. It would tear me apart; my heart literally wouldn't be able to handle it. I washed my face with cold water then patted it dry.

Chapter 6

Me and Cameron joined our father in the truck, he drove us to our grandparents. Our father didn't stay long. He hugged us, unloaded our luggage, and left. Our grandparents were eager to get us settled in. It had been years since we visited their home, it was truly beautiful. Every room was a work of art, immaculate described it perfectly. We picked out our rooms then joined them in the dining hall for dinner.

We sat down; they handed us a sheet of paper. We opened it to find a set of rules. We hated rules, our own parents didn't have rules for us. We were always able to do whatever we wanted when we wanted. Our grandparents made it clear that if we disobeyed, we would be punished. We hadn't been there for an hour; they were off to a bad start. If the living arrangement was going to work, we had to be comfortable.

I asked to be excused. I went to my bedroom and destroyed the artwork on the walls. I hoped while we were at school the following day, they would discover it and kick us out. I no longer had an appetite. My stomach was upset, I was angry we had to leave one bootcamp and join another. I called my friend Sasha, we talked for hours. Luckily, she helped me feel better.

It was indeed a shitty situation, but I had to make the best of it. I thought by the move to our grandparents we no longer worked for our parents but that wasn't the case. I still hadn't found my cellphone. I had to buy another one, I went to my brother's room and asked to borrow his for a little while. Just when I grabbed it our father sent a screenshot of my cellphone. I thought earlier I was certain of where I left mines, but he found it outside in the grill on the patio. He drove to us so I could have it.

I checked my email and found a list of people me and Cameron were ordered to execute soon. There were four people on the list. Two of the names I knew. They were my best friends Sasha brothers. I sighed, Cameron asked what was wrong with me. I didn't say anything, I simply pointed at the names on the list. He recognized the names too, he said "it's either them or us sis".

He pulled out the black box our mother had given to us earlier, I took it from him and threw it out the window. He shoved me and jumped out the window onto the roof. I ran to the window and tried to get him to come back in, but he wouldn't. I then told him if we got in trouble, he'd better sleep with one eye opened. Nothing I said bothered him. I had to get to that box before he did. We were supposed to be in bed but instead I had to find a way out the house without making any noise.

The security system installed would sound if I opened any one of the doors. I ran back upstairs to Cameron's room. My only way out the house was through the window. I joined my brother on the roof. I was so pissed at him that I shut the window not realizing it locked from the inside. I scooted my way across the roof until I got close enough to him. We fought and it was a matter of time our grandparents awakened.

The fight ended with him falling off the roof and me falling through it. The fall sprained both our ankles. Cameron was in too much pain to notice the box was inches away from him. Surprisingly, the ruckus didn't wake our grandmother and grandfather. I held on to a stool I had come across and pulled myself up. My ankle hurt like hell and so did my chest from the fall. I fell hard as hell, I prayed I didn't break anything.

When I found my way out the piano room I held on to the walls and hopped to the front door. Beside it was a window. I opened the blinds, and my brother still hadn't moved. I could tell he was in agony. I closed the blinds and hopped up forty-five steps. When at the top I had to rest my ankle for a moment. A few minutes later I held on to the walls once again until I made it to Cameron's room.

I unlocked the window and proceeded towards the roof again. I crawled until I reached the edge. I looked down and had to close my eyes. It was too high; I was afraid of heights. My brother cried out to me, I told him to hold on, I would figure out something. I sat on the edge of the roof and thought if I jumped down with him, we would be stuck outside. We wouldn't have a way to get back inside if we were both stranded in the front yard.

We desperately needed medical attention. I called my father for the passcode to the alarm system. He didn't know it, he woke our mother to ask her, she knew it. He told me the numbers. I went back inside and found the security system. The system was adjacent to our grandparents' room. I pressed the first number, and it was loud as hell. I waited a little to see if any movement would come from their room, but it didn't.

I proceeded with the next three numbers. The doors unlocked and I ran as best as I could to the front lawn. I dragged Cameron inside and closed the door. He was still in a great deal of pain. I took off one of his shoes and stuffed his sock in his mouth. He took it out and screamed. I slapped him.

I went to the kitchen and got an icepack out the freezer. I ran to him and dropped it on his face. Although, I was nursing him back to health, I was still very angry with him. I wished I could've brainwashed him, but he had to live his own life. I ran back to the kitchen and found another roll of duct tape; I couldn't find the one I had prior. I took the icepack off Cameron's face and placed it on his sprained ankle and wrapped the tape around it a few times. It didn't help, I feared he had to go to the hospital more than I did.

I turned the kitchen light off and dragged my brother up the stairs to his bedroom and put him into bed. He apologized to me for what he did. He begged me not to snitch on him, I assured him that wouldn't happen in a million years. I turned the ceiling fan on for him and turned off the lights. I then went to my bedroom and went to bed. Hours passed and I still hadn't gone to sleep. Finally, I got out the bed, went down the hall, and watched movies until it was time for school.

I showered and got dressed for school. My brother was in no position to move, let alone go to school. Our grandparents called us over the intercom to come down for breakfast. I paced back and forth in Cameron's room; I had no idea how I could cover for him. They would find out rather quickly due to the damage we caused. When twenty minutes passed and we still hadn't gone downstairs, our grandmother came to us. She knocked on Cameron's door.

We both starred at the door afraid to open it. When stressed I had a habit of biting my nails, I bit them to the point they bled. I opened the door and she pushed me out the way. I stumbled a little then caught my balance. She was furious Cameron was still in bed. She pulled back the covers and saw his ankle. All I thought was "damn".

She charged towards me yelling. I placed both my hands over my ears. I was annoyed by her voice. Whenever she got angry, the pitch of her voice changed. I tried to explain what happened, but her anger prevented her from hearing me. She stormed past me and called our grandfather. He finished his breakfast then went upstairs.

By this time our grandmother had discovered the hole in the roof of the piano room. I ran into my grandfather coming up the stairs. I didn't want to stay to hear what she had to say. He okayed me to go to school. I had no idea how I would get there with no vehicle. My grandfather let my arms go and I followed him downstairs. He went into their bedroom and came out with a key.

I drove my grandfather's Lincoln to school. I loved the heated, leathery seats. I got a phone call from principal Jenkins when I got inside. He informed me of his whereabouts. He was out the hospital and home with his wife. He wanted me to stop by, he needed to give me something he said. I went to all my classes and handed my teachers the assignments they needed from me then left.

Thirty minutes later I arrived at my principal's home. I went inside and he handed me a folded picture. I unfolded it and saw twins. I didn't understand why he wanted me to have that picture. I knew the officer who arrested me and my brother that late night had a twin brother. Principal Jenkins pointed at one of the brothers, I noticed he was missing four of his fingers on his right hand. I then understood why I needed that photo.

On the back of the photo was an address to Officer Wilks place. I finished out the remainder of the day of school at principal Jenkins's house. I was too drunk to drive but I drove anyway when I left. I picked William, Tony, and his sister Lily up from school and dropped them off at their houses. I then inputted the address on the back of the photo into GPS. Officer Wilks didn't live far from Tony and Lily. The drive was eight minutes.

I drove by the house slowly and saw both twins. A black van sped past me and pulled into the driveway. Three men with orange ski-masks and ak-47 riffles kicked in the front door. An innocent family gathering turned into a horror show. It appeared Officer Wilks family had no idea the family man was involved with illegal substances. I parked my grandfather Lincoln down the block. I had to get inside and execute everyone.

The front door was left open. I snuck inside; the family had been taken into the basement. I had to act fast. I had to be the one who executed Officer Wilks. My brother and I deserved justice. I didn't care about anyone else, but they were extras. I couldn't leave behind any witnesses. Although their names weren't on my parents list, the more people I murdered, the happier my parents were.

I had to get to the basement, but I was too thirsty to pursue it at that precise moment. I crawled to the refrigerator and drank a little apple juice, I then tiptoed to the basement door. It too was left open. I pulled my gun from the hoister and looked down the steps into the basement, but I didn't see anyone at first. It wasn't until I crept down a few steps I saw Officer Wilks Tied to a chair. Before I pulled the trigger, I looked at both his hands. I was certain I had the right target; I didn't see any of his fingers missing.

I decided not to shoot officer Wilks first without killing the others first. It would've been impossible for me to get out the house in time and make it to the car. It wouldn't have taken much for them to catch up to my chubby ass. One man was in the bathroom. I shot the handle of the bathroom door. The man jumped up from the toilet, ran out screaming like a little girl. I shot him first.

The other men pointed their weapons at me but before anyone pulled their triggers, I had shot them all. Officer Wilks and his brother misunderstood the scenario.

They thought I was there to rescue them. I was pissed the officer didn't recognize my face, but I expected that from him. I untied him and the two brothers were happy they were free again, well so they thought. They got halfway up the stairs and I hadn't moved. Officer Wilks turned around and asked me if I would join them for dinner.

I stared at him blanky then responded. I told him I wouldn't have dinner with him if he and I were the last two people on earth. He didn't understand why I was sarcastic towards him. They proceeded up the steps, I stopped them. I had nothing to say to Officer Wilks, he would never know how badly he hurt us that night. Without hesitation I shot him. His brother had no idea what was going on.

I explained why I did what I did. He asked if I was going to kill him too. He begged me not to. I told him it was nothing personal, I couldn't leave behind any witnesses. I shot him; the two brothers died side by side. I was overwhelmed with anger that on my way out the basement I shot Officer Wilks an additional forty-five times. I then did something I thought I would never do. I cut his penis off and shoved it into his mouth, I wanted humiliated even in death.

I ran out the house down the street to my grandfather's car. My brother called to inform me of the punishment they had given us. I started the car and put him on speaker phone. While I drove back to our grandparent's home, my brother informed me we were grounded for three months. Neither myself nor my brother could live isolated from civilization for three months. We hung up from each other and I sped to their house. My grandfather snatched the keys from me quicker than I could turn off the car.

My grandfather pulled me out his car and pushed me until we were inside the house. He slammed the door and told me how much the damages were both me and Cameron caused. I smirked at him, reached into my pocket, pulled out a joint, and lit it. The disrespect angered my grandparents more. My grandfather snatched the blunt from my hand, threw it on the ground, and stepped on it. That pissed me off, he wasted my weed. That was unacceptable.

I walked away from him while he was still yelling and stormed upstairs to my brother's room. I was too heated to speak at first. I had to sit down and calm myself. It took me quite a while to get my emotions together. When I felt better, I told him we had to go back to mom and dad. I couldn't stand another day there, he explained in the meantime we had no choice. We didn't have anywhere to go.

All I knew was things were getting worse, not better. We loved our grandparents, but we had to get the hell out of there. I walked to Cameron's closet and opened it. There was a trunk full of CD's, I grabbed one, turned on the CD player, and played it. I turned the volume on the stereo as loud as it would go to anger our grandparents furthermore. It was only so much they could handle, especially at their ages. I strongly believed it was a matter of time they would kick us out.

My friend Sasha called, I answered. I was hesitant at first, I hated her brother was someone I had to execute. He was an intelligent, outgoing, courageous, and funny guy. The saddest part was his twenty first birthday was in a few days. I heard what my friend had to say. I was on the verge of ending the call. She told me she knew exactly what I was up to. I pretended I had no idea what she meant by that.

Sasha informed me her brother knew my parents wanted him dead. She pleaded with me not to do the deed. I explained to her that I didn't have a choice, if I didn't execute him me and Cameron would have a hit placed on our heads. I ended the call before she finished her last statement, then I thought I needed to get her brothers whereabouts. Finding him would've been much easier. I called her back, she answered on the first ring. I lied and told her our last call dropped and that I needed my cellphone fixed.

Sasha's brother whereabouts were unknown. He didn't trust anyone after he found out a lot of people wanted him dead. He didn't even trust his sister or their parents anymore. I ended the call; I didn't want to hear shit else she had to say. I loved my friend and her family, but the money blinded me. Neither myself nor my brother could allow our emotions to interfere with business. I had to find out where her brother was, I didn't have much time.

I went downstairs to the kitchen and poured me a glass of grape juice. Our grandparents were still angry with us. Frankly, neither one of us cared. The doorbell rang a few times. I looked at my granny and she looked at me, apparently, she didn't want to know who it was. I ran to the front door and answered it. It was my father.

He had the chevy he had given me and Cameron in the driveway. I was happy because we needed the car. I hugged my father, took the keys, went inside to my bedroom and got a jacket, then met him back outside. On the drive back to his house he wanted to know if me and Cameron executed any of the three men on his list. My progression made my father a happy man that evening. He sensed something was on my mind, he wanted me to share whatever it was with him. I took a deep breath and told him.

I hated Cameron was bed bound a few days due to his ankle, but he couldn't take credit for hits he didn't help me with. When we arrived at the house my father told me he understood. Cameron of course wouldn't be punished for his lack of participation since he was temporarily injured. He then proceeded to tell me my share was a million bucks for all three executions. I was extremely satisfied. After all I did deserve it. I worked hard for that money.

I went into the house with my father. My mother was asleep on the sofa. I walked over to her and kissed her on her cheek. The kiss awakened her. I told her I wouldn't be there long, she hugged me and asked how my stay was so far at her husband's parents. I looked at my father, I sensed there was tension in the air. I didn't know why, and I didn't care to know why.

My father made out a check to me. When he handed it to me my heartbeat began to race, and my eyes widened. Before I left, I asked my father if he knew where my friend Sasha's brother would go. He had no idea, and I had no idea how I would find him. I drove back to my grandparents. The roof had been finally fixed and they finally were calm. I took the elevator to Cameron's room.

Chapter 7

My plan was to show him the check, but he was in the bathroom. I sat on his bed and waited for him for thirty minutes. When he came out, I waved the check in his face. He wanted to know where his check was. I told him he wasn't getting one for the three hits since he couldn't help me. He was pissed as I knew he would be. I told him I would spend some more time with him whenever he calmed down. I left his room and went to mines.

I went outside onto my balcony and drank a little of the pina colada rum I had left over. It was delicious. I wasn't much of a drinker but when I tasted that for the first time, it made me want to drink more. I called another good friend of mines and asked her if she knew where Sasha's brother Vincent was. Gina was his ex-girlfriend and she always kept eyes on him in the streets. She knew exactly where he was, I ran into my room and grabbed a pin and pad.

Gina informed me Vincent was at a pool hall in Arlington. I wrote down the address and asked her a few questions. She answered them all to the best of her knowledge. Before I ended the call, I told her I would meet her early the next morning before school. She wanted to know why. As I hung up, I told her again to meet me. I called my parents and informed them where Vincent would be the next day at precisely noon until eight at night.

I asked my parents if they wanted to join me at the pool hall when it was time to pay a visit to Vincent. They had no desire join me, but they wanted to still see the action from the comfort of their bed. I laughed, I assured them I would most definitely film it for them. I had a new camera that I hadn't used, I couldn't wait to watch the murder on the big screen. Every murder to me was the perfect murder. The more I did it, the easier it became. I had a natural gnat for it.

I woke up the next morning and met Gina at a seven-eleven. When I spotted her car, I pulled up beside her, got out, and got in the passenger seat of her vehicle. I surprised her with a couple grand in cash. She became ecstatic, she wasn't expecting that much from me. I told her it was because of her that I could execute another person on my parents hit list. She agreed, took the money, then hugged me. I then got out her car and went into the gas station.

When I went inside a girl around my age caught my eye. I figured she had to go to Arlington High since she wasn't far from the school. Her hair was long and jet black, lips were juicy, and her fat was in all the right places. I approached her and introduced myself. She flirted back and introduced herself. Her name was Silvia. I starred deeply into her eyes.

Silva's eyes were gray, same color as my brother's. I reached into my back pocket and pulled out my cellphone. We exchanged numbers, purchased a few snacks, and walked each other out the store. I sensed she was a bit shy, so was I. She ran to a white truck and got in the passenger seat. There was a man behind the wheel, I figured he was her father. I couldn't see his face.

I got in my car and trailed the white truck to Arlington High. There were butterflies in my stomach when I first met her. I wanted a friendship as well as a beautiful romance. She was the prettiest girl in school. After her father dropped her off, I walked her to her first class. I grabbed her ass on her way inside. She yelled at me as if she didn't like that, but her body language told me a different story.

Silvia was drop dead gorgeous. It was her first day and every guy wanted her. I had to work harder and faster if I wanted a chance to date her. My plan after school was to take her shopping and have dinner afterwards. I went to my classes and turned in the assignments that were due at the time. My teachers were upset that I stopped going to class for a little time, but I saw no issue with it if I stayed on top of things. When I met with Mr. Jones, he wanted to have a "little talk" with me, I sighed and rolled my eyes.

I stood in the hallway for over an hour listening to Mr. Jones. I thought to myself how hot his breath was. I wondered if he owned a toothbrush and if he ever used one. He never caught the hint that it was extremely unpleasant for me to stand there any longer. I turned my head and ran for the door. He chased after me but by the time he made it to the front door of the school I was already in my car, started it, and sped off the parking lot.

Principal Jenkins wife called me. She informed me he would be returning to school before the week was over. I was thrilled, he was by far the coolest principal I ever had. She also added the withdrawals were kicking his ass and that he needed more coke. Her words saddened me, I hated the fact he loved hard-core drugs and that he got my brother hooked on that shit. I had to take care of them though. I couldn't make the choice for them to stop.

I drove to my grandparents and snuck into my brother's room. His little black box was on his night-stand next to his bed. All I had to do was grab it and run. I gently closed his door so I wouldn't wake him. I then tiptoed to the left side of his bed and grabbed the box. I looked down and starred at him. He was always a loud snorer and he always slept with his mouth opened, I hated that.

I ran out my brother's room downstairs. I placed my hand on the knob to open the door, my grandpa startled me.

He asked why I wasn't in school. I informed him I was one of the four smartest students in the school. He had no idea how that related to his question. I added that I was well ahead in all my classes. In fact, I was so ahead that I had already completed all the assignments for the school year, I chose to turn them in when they were due.

My response satisfied my grandpa. I ran out the house and drove to the pool hall Gina informed me of. I arrived at a place called Clicks Billiards. In my opinion it was the best pool halls in town. My parents knew everyone who usually hung out at the place and because of this me and my brother could get in for free. However, we hadn't been there in years. I had seen a few changes had been made to the place.

I went inside the club, most things had been changed, but I still knew my way around. Everyone greeted me. They wanted me to hangout for a while, I assured them I would after I handled some business. A few fellas hugged me and shook my hand, they wanted to know if I needed their help with anything. I smiled evilly and told them who I was there for. One of the fellas pulled me closer and whispered, "Vincent is in the back baby girl, if you need my gun, you can use mines". I pulled away from him and whispered, "I got my own shit, but thanks anyway".

I pulled a curtain back and saw Vincent and a woman pleasing each other orally. I stood there a minute and watched. I wasn't turned on, I thought of way I could and should've killed them. They were oblivious of my presence; I wanted their attention. I went into my wallet and pulled out fifty cents. I threw the two quarters at their heads, my presence feared them both. Ironically Vincent thought the pool hall was the safest haven for him, he thought everyone there would protect him.

I smiled and said, "a lot of people know me, and I know a lot of people", with that being said, everyone here will protect me". Vincent backed up from me and stood by his new girlfriend. I paced the floor with a knife in my hands behind my back. I walked towards them and raised my knife. They continued to step back and screamed but I had no intentions to kill them at that moment, I backed up and laughed at them. I then went into my backpack, opened the camera, and turned it on. I couldn't forget to film whatever I planned for my parents to see.

I called the boss of the club to join us in the private room. I informed him of the camera and my parents. He waived at it and told them how much he missed them. I then picked up the camera and put it on Vincent. I asked him if he had anything to say to my parents, he laughed and pulled out a gun and shot himself. I then shot his girlfriend to make up for not being able to murder Vincent. We had a big mess on our hands.

The boss of the club and I double wrapped their bodies in garbage bags then tapped them. I grabbed the camera, turned it off, and placed it into my backpack. The boss stepped out the room and alerted everyone to keep watch while we dispose of the bodies. However, when he returned, I didn't have to lift a finger. His crew had taken care of everything, and I didn't have to worry about them fucking it up. They were professionals, they worked closely with my parents sometimes. My brother and I were introduced to them at an extremely young age, I was six and Cameron was 7 when we first seen a dead body.

Once business had been taken care of, I had been invited to play a game of pool. I couldn't stay, instead I took a beer to go. I waited to drink it at principal Jenkins's house. He and his wife thought I had shown up empty-handed. They were relieved when I showed them where the cocaine was hidden. I then had given them the box and they were free to do as much as they wanted in my presence until I left. I wondered if Cameron was still asleep, I had to return the box before he noticed it was missing.

I chatted with principal Jenkins and his wife for a few hours. When I realized what time, it was and decided to leave. They didn't want me to leave, they wanted more coke. My patience had run out with them, I was irritated. I allowed them access to the best coke in town for a few hours and that still wasn't enough. I snatched the box and grabbed my car keys off their coffee table. I didn't bother to explain how I felt, they were too high to understand.

I drove back to my grandparents. On my way I stopped and grabbed a bite to eat for Cameron just in case if he was awake upon my arrival. Twenty minutes after I arrived at my grandparents to find my brother sitting in a lawn chair in the driveway. I could see his ankle was better and I could see he was agitated. I didn't want to fight. We made eye contact and he charged towards the car. I bypassed the house and circled around the block eight times.

I pulled into the driveway and grabbed the remote for the garage door and opened it. I then pulled inside and closed the door. I got out and rambled through my belongings for the key to the back door. I couldn't find it; I had no choice but to ring the doorbell. I rang the doorbell and Cameron answered it. he wouldn't let me inside without giving him the coke first. Since he wanted to be an asshole, I pulled out the box, opened it, and threw the rest of it in his face.

My brother at that point was a true addict. I glanced back at him on my way to the elevator and he was on the floor scraping up as much of the coke as he could. The elevator opened and I pressed the number three for the third floor. I got stuck on the second floor. I yelled for my grandparents, but no one came. I then called for my brother to rescue me, but I was afraid he wouldn't come due to what I had done upon my entrance. Thankfully, after I yelled for him a few times he came for me.

He kicked the elevator numerous times in hopes it would drop down to the first floor. Our grandparents heard the ruckus and ran to us. They informed me I would have to wait a while for someone to come fix it. Grandpa ran downstairs and found a list of contacts he could call. There were many handy men in the family, at least twenty me and Cameron knew of. A few minutes later grandpa came upstairs and told us a guy named Rufus would meet them. I was thrilled, it was hot as hell in that elevator.

Five hours passed and I was still trapped in the elevator. I didn't want to spend my entire Saturday trapped. The doorbell rang, grandpa yelled for them to come in. Rufus met us on the second floor with a toolbox. It was a glass elevator, but the glass was too thick for anyone to break. Rufus got an idea and ran to his truck. He came back with a bazooka.

He was the only one in town who owned one. He pointed at the elevator, we yelled for him not to shoot that thing. It would kill us all; we had a good laugh. Rufus placed the bazooka on the ground and went into his toolbox. He pulled out a crowbar. He used it to pry the doors open. It took him an hour to pry the doors open just enough for me to get through.

I squeezed through the opening and yelled "Hallelujah"! I sweated out the curls I had, I had a date with Silvia that night and I had no idea who I could call to do my hair. I held on to my grandma's arm and walked with her to the bathroom on the second floor. She rinsed a washcloth for me with cold water and placed it on my face. I was extremely hot; it took a few cold rinses for me to feel better. I hugged my granny and thanked her for her help. We then rejoined the others down the hall.

I hugged my grandpa for helping me as well. I looked around for Rufus, but I didn't see him. I asked my grandparents where he was, and they told me he was about to leave. I rushed downstairs. He attempted to start his car, but each attempt was failed. Now he was trapped outside. I told my grandparents what had happened, and they rushed down with me and met him outside.

I thanked Rufus for his help. I looked in the passenger seat and saw his bazooka. I wanted to purchase it. I had to have it. Cameron joined us outside. He starred at the bazooka as I did, then he looked at me. We communicated through our eyes, as we usually did whenever our grandparents were around.

Our grandpa had looked at Rufus engine. He concluded he needed a new one, but he didn't have enough money to purchase one. He might as well had bought him a new car. My grandpa opened the garage door and invited Rufus inside. He asked him which car did he like the most. Rufus pointed to a 1974 blue Nova. Me and Cameron watched our grandfather give him the keys and the car. We weren't shocked that he did that, our grandparents cared a lot for people, in fact they cared a bit too much and sometimes it was their downfall.

We helped Rufus remove all his belongings from his truck and placed them into the Nova. When our grandparents left our presence, we asked Rufus if the bazooka was for sale. It wasn't, but for us he was willing to sell it. He wanted ten grand for it, that was well below what we expected him to say granted the history of it. Cameron ran upstairs and grabbed a bag full of money. We didn't know how much was inside, but we knew it was more than enough. I handed the bag to Rufus, and he handed me the bazooka, it was the first time I ever held one, it was heavy as hell.

I threw the bazooka at Cameron and waved goodbye to Rufus as he backed out the driveway. I ran inside and joined our grandparents for lunch while Cameron stayed in the front yard with the bazooka. He had taken pictures of him holding it and posted them onto his Facebook and Instagram pages. I scrolled through his pages and liked all his pictures. My mind was racing, I couldn't wait to blow up some shit. I'm sure my brother thought the same. For our next kill we would use it.

My brother joined us in the kitchen for lunch, shortly after his cellphone rang. He answered, he couldn't get more than two words out without our father yelling at him. He was pissed at Cameron for posting those pictures. He wanted him to take them down, but Cameron wouldn't do it. What made matters worse was he ended the call prior to our father finishing his thoughts. Shortly after my cellphone rang. I ignored the calls; my actions would have consequences.

Our grandparents wanted to know what the hype was all about. We didn't tell them; we knew if we had of another argument would've started. Me and Cameron tried to engage in conversation with them over lunch but no matter how hard we tried, things remained awkward. We ate our meal in silence. When we finished, I went around the table and grabbed the plates and silverware. I placed everything in the dishwasher and turned it on. Just as me and Cameron were leaving the kitchen messages from our dad poured to his parent's cellphones, he sent them everything Cameron posted and my comments of every picture and status followed.

Lunch ended with our grandparents furious at us. We just knew they would kick us out, but they didn't, instead they sent us to church for prayer. We spent the remainder of our weekend in church. The next morning, we weren't allowed to go to school due to our punishment. We had to clean every inch of the mansion until we were freed of our sins, we didn't understand their concept. The life we lived we would always be sinners, but we told them whatever they needed to hear. We scrubbed everything for hours on end, we had to take a break, we hadn't eaten anything since lunch the day before.

We ran to the kitchen and snuck some food. We dropped all we had soon as we turned around, our grandparents wouldn't allow us to eat until they wanted us to. I could feel my stomach twisting into a knot. We were both starving, we had to find another way to get food. We went back to cleaning windows. A few minutes after our granny returned with a couple chains. She wrapped them around the freezer and refrigerator handle and placed a lock on it.

Me and Cameron continued to clean as our grandparents cut off our access to food in the kitchen. I cried, at that point I felt starvation would kill me faster than a bullet would in the streets. Six hours later we decided to quit cleaning everything. We went to our rooms, showered, and changed clothes. I joined my brother in his room once he was settled. He called his friend Tony and explained what our grandparents had done. An hour later Tony arrived at our grandparent's mansion with two philly cheese steak subs, fries, and a couple drinks.

Chapter 8

Tony and Lily parked down the street. We didn't understand why his sister was with him when my brother specifically told him to come alone. I glanced out my brother's window and saw Lily and Tony running down the street. Me and Camron ran downstairs. I inputted the security code, and my brother quietly opened the front door. We invited them inside. I sensed they were drunk, both Lily and her brother words were slurred.

We grabbed our food and they followed us to my bedroom. My brother asked Tony why he brought his sister with him. His response was Lily wanted to get out the house for a little while, while their grandparents were asleep. My brother looked at me and shook his head. Although he was agitated with Tony, he dropped the matter. I then thanked them for the food and turned on the game. I picked up a controller and so did Lily.

Lily and I chose our characters then started the game. I fought her in wrestling match and won. She couldn't or wouldn't accept her fate. We rematched six times and each time I won. She wanted to play a seventh time, but I ended the game and chatted with my brother and Tony. Our conversation regarded our principal. Principal Jenkins needed an intervention, and soon. He had to stop doing coke.

Me and Cameron pranked called a few people. Every person we called threatened to kill us. After the last call we all heard loud music outside. We ran to my window and opened it. We saw Sasha and two others. They tissued and egged the house. Sasha was angry that her brother Vincent was killed.

She had no idea he killed himself. The commotion outside eventually awakened my granny and grandpa. They rushed outside and made a desperate attempt to get rid of them. Their attempts didn't work. The police were called, then Cameron and I were called downstairs. Our grandparents were so angry they kicked us out. We were happy, that's exactly what we wanted them to do.

We thought we'd never see the day they got fed up. Me and Cameron were called downstairs. They called us before we could sneak Lily and Tony out. They hid in my closet. When we were in our grandparent's sight, they informed us they knew we had company over. They wanted us to call them down. I yelled for them to come downstairs; they had taken their sweet time.

Sasha and her crew fled the scene before cops arrived. Our grandparents called our parents and let them know they kicked us out. Tony and Lily finally met us downstairs. They were sent home. Meanwhile, me and Cameron stood and listened to our grandparents go on and on about how we were demon seeds. We understood their level of anger granted all we put them through, but they didn't have to worry about us damaging anything further in their home. When they finished, they sent us to our rooms to pack our belongings.

When we finished packing, we packed our things into our car. Our grandparents hugged us and wished us well with all our future endeavors. I held them tightly for a few minutes, leaving was bittersweet. Me and Cameron kissed them on their cheek, turned around, and left. We waved goodbye and blasted the music on our way down the road. Cameron drove us to his friend William's house. We relaxed there for a few hours then went home.

As me and Cameron decided to leave William's house, we decided to spend the night. We weren't ready to see our parents yet. Sasha and her friends were taken downtown by authorities and questioned. They denied they had anything to do with tissuing and egging our grandparent's home. Early the next morning I woke up before the others. I went into the living room and turned on the television. I couldn't believe what I heard.

I ran to Williams room and awakened my brother. As he wiped his eyes, he told me I better had a good reason to wake him. I grabbed one of his arms and pulled him to the living room, I then grabbed the remote control and unmuted the news. Cameron wiped his eyes once more and listened. Sasha and her friends escaped from authorities. They returned to our grandparent's home, broke in, and killed them. We left our belongings behind and drove to the scene.

When I turned on our grandparent's street there were sixteen squad cars. I paralleled parked in front of a neighbor's home. We ran towards the house and an officer wouldn't allow us to pass. I informed the officer of who we were to the victims. He allowed us to pass. We walked slowly, my brother and I couldn't bare the agony. I glanced at Cameron; he didn't look well. He leaned over and threw up.

I had given Cameron the napkin in my pocket and patted his back. He wiped his mouth and followed me inside. A detective asked us who we were. We introduced ourselves then followed her to our grandparent's bedroom. They laid side by side with over two hundred stab wounds. I ran out while Cameron starred at them. When outside a detective stopped me and asked if my grandparents had any enemies.

Tears had fallen down my cheeks. My grandparents had no enemies I responded. I then said the names of the four assailants. Detective Frost wrote the names in his note pad. My brother joined me outside. Both our cellphones rang, mom called me, and dad called Cameron. I quickly explained everything.

They hated we weren't there at the time of the murders. We could've stopped them. We hung up from our parents and drove home. We met them in the kitchen. Cameron and I pulled out a stool and sat down at the counter. I told our parents everything we knew about Sasha and her friends. We didn't know much about her friends, but we knew once we found Sasha, we would find her friends.

Our father called Sasha's father. Their friendship was ten years strong. He could easily find her whereabouts. He pressed the speaker phone so we could all hear. Mr. Jackson answered, Sasha left his home a few minutes prior to the call. She was headed to her friend Malik's house where she would find her other two friends Freddy and Rena. Her father had given the address of Malik's home.

Dad started the car. Mom sat in the passenger seat, as for me and Cameron, we sat in the back. Dad drove to the address as if he was a maniac. We understood the hostile aggression. We arrived at the same time as Sasha. As she turned into the driveway, she starred at the strange all white Mercedes Benz. She couldn't see us due to the dark tinted windows.

Mom and dad got out the car, they wouldn't allow us to partake in the kills. We sat still and stared out Cameron's window. Sasha ran to the front door of Maliks house. She banged on the door in a desperate attempt to alert her friend, but Malik was in her bedroom cleaning her bathroom and the others had a gaming headset on. Once mom and dad were close enough, dad shot Sasha in the back of her head, and mom shot her in her back. Malik heard the gunshots and ran towards the front door. Rena removed her headset and went to the bathroom.

Rena saw Malik. She called her name, but Malik didn't answer. Dad kicked down the door, Malik froze and was shot in the throat. Rena ran and alerted Freddy. Mom and dad stepped inside the house. Dad searched downstairs while mom searched upstairs. They found no one. Cameron and I saw Rena and Freddy run pass the car and around the corner.

Dad searched the backyard and found a puppy. He picked it up and went back inside. Mom joined him, they walked slowly as they played with the puppy to the car. They got inside and told us of their extraordinary kills. They were thrilled. They thought they had killed everyone involved, but they were wrong as can be. I took my cellphone out and messaged Cameron, I said "since they didn't allow us to partake in the kills, we will have our own thrill kill as well!"

Mom drove us home. Mom ran to the kitchen and popped a bottle of champagne. Her and dad celebrated while me and Cameron plotted how we would kill Rena and Freddy. I remembered where Freddy lived. That was all I needed. We ran downstairs, our parents were so caught up in themselves they didn't notice us leave. Ten minutes later we arrived at Freddy's house. His mom had just come home with groceries.

He helped her take them inside. I reached under the driver seat and grabbed a Glock our dad left behind. We got out the car and ran towards the home. We hid behind his mother's truck. When outside again she walked to the truck and screamed when she saw us. I shot her once in her vagina, that alone sent her to the ground. She held her crotch while she laid face down.

I handed Cameron the gun, he shot her execution style. Freddy and Rena heard the gunshots. They headed for the back door. We were inside before they had a chance to escape. Cameron shot at them twice and missed. The third shot pierced Rena's heart. Cameron handed me the gun.

I chased Freddy throughout the house. When I got tired, I demanded he come down and take it like a man. He tiptoed to the last room on the left. I walked slowly with both hands on the gun up the stairs. I pointed when I reached the hallway. I checked every room. The last room was the one on the left.

I placed my hand on the doorknob and opened it. Freddy opened the window and ran onto the roof. I ran to the window and looked out. I saw Freddy and shot him in the back of his right leg. He fell to the ground. I then climbed out the window and ran to him. He grabbed my left ankle, he wanted me to help him.

I stood over him and saw he peed on himself. I then pointed the gun at his head, placed my hand on the trigger, and pulled. His brains flew everywhere. I then walked back to the window he opened. I went inside and closed the window. Me and Cameron ran out the house and drove to his friend William's. Cameron cried as his friend comforted him.

I went inside the trailer and sat across from his grandfather. I stared at the television while he stared at me. I then grabbed the remote controller and muted it. I whispered and asked him what he wanted me to know about William. The old man reached for his eyeglasses on the lamp stand next to him. He then placed them on his eyes and simply said "William and little boys". He then placed them back on the lamp stand.

I unmuted the television and handed William's grandfather the remote. As I walked past the old man, he grabbed my hand and said, "protect the children" and fell asleep. I didn't know if the old man was crazy or if William usually molested young boys. Although I was conflicted with the issue, I would get to the bottom of it. What's done in the dark always comes to light. If what his grandfather said was true, I would expose him to my brother. The old man held my wrist tightly while he was asleep, I pulled away from him and walked to the kitchen sink.

My brother and William joined me in the kitchen. I leaned over the sink and turned the faucet on. The cold water splashed onto my face was exactly what I needed to gather my thoughts. My brother sensed I wasn't myself. William had taken a sip of water and excused himself so we could have a moment alone. My brother followed me outside. I reached in my back pocket and pulled out my cellphone.

I then motioned my hand for him to come closer. I played the brief conversation between myself and William's grandfather. We listened in; we were both overwhelmed. Cameron snatched my phone and ran to Williams room. His door was locked. Cameron quietly picked the lock while William blasted his music. When William saw him, he was surprised and when my brother saw William he was surprised.

William turned his music off and Cameron played the recording from my phone for him. William listened in and afterwards denied the accusation. My brother stared at him, disgusted of what he heard, William's naked appearance was overlooked. I grabbed my phone from my brother and placed it in the left side of my bra. Cameron then said to William "man if that's what you do and you supposed to be my friend, I will make sure you die a slow horrific death". William never changed his answer. He walked towards Cameron, hugged him and said, "if you can't trust me by now and I am one of your dearest friends then shame on you my brother".

My brother pulled away from William and said, "we'll see how good of a friend you truly are." He then grabbed our belongings we left behind. I took my backpack from Cameron, walked outside, and started the car. I threw my backpack in the back seat and shifted the gear to reverse. Cameron ran out, he thought I was going to leave without him. I opened my window, leaned out and told him to hold on a minute. I backed out the driveway then backed in.

Cameron got inside and I sped off. I watched William cry in my rearview mirror. When I turned the corner, I asked Cameron what he had in mind for William. In response he said "my question should've been what he had in mind for William, Tony, and Lily. I then asked and he told me we would test their loyalty. My brother then added soon we would have our own crew and we wouldn't have to work for our parents anymore. The thought of that had given me a moment of relief then fear.

We stopped at KFC on our way home and ordered an eight-piece chicken dinner with a side of mac and cheese and cold slaw. We ate our portion on the way home. When we arrived the gate to the backyard was opened. I parked the car and mom met us outside. I handed her the food and asked if dad was burying something in the backyard. She wouldn't answer my question. Cameron ran to our father and asked, he too wouldn't answer.

Mom joined dad in the backyard while me and Cameron went into the house. We put our belongings into our rooms and investigated. A few minutes in the search we found a trail of blood. It led us to the garage door. I stared at the blood and wondered who it belonged to. Cameron opened the garage door, there were two bodies on the ground. The bodies were wrapped in a white blanket.

I ran to the kitchen and grabbed a pair of scissors on the counter. Cameron tried to unwrap the bodies, but he couldn't get the duct tape off. I stopped him and ran back into the garage. I used the scissors to cut an opening at their heads so we could see their faces. We saw the first face and screamed, then the second. I ran to the backyard, Cameron ran to the car and sped off. I wanted answers of why our grandparents were wrapped in blankets in the garage and why a proper funeral wasn't in place for them.

My dad finally answered me when he finished digging their graves. He ranted on and on of how he hated his mother and father and how they never appreciated him and his wife's accomplishments. It was a hard pill to swallow and although I understood my father's anger towards them, he was dead wrong. My grandparents may not have loved them, but they loved me and Cameron to death and I wished we could've laid them to rest the right way. I stepped back and watched him throw his parents into their graves. I looked at mother and she didn't look my way until father finished. He threw the shovel at me as if I was a target on his hitlist.

I bent down; the shovel missed me by a few inches. I had no words as I watched mom and dad walk hand in hand into the house. I was left in the backyard; all I could do was stare at the graves. I walked closer and said my final goodbye, I told them mother and father would pay for what they've done one way or another. I wiped the tears from my eyes and heard Cameron pull into the driveway. I didn't care the music was too loud for me to hear my thoughts. I didn't want to think of what our parents had done.

Cameron got out the car, ran to his room, and packed a few bags. There was no need for me to tell him what happened, he already knew when he no longer saw the bodies in the garage. I ran to my room and did the same. I then met Cameron back in his room and closed the door. I asked him what the plan was, of course he didn't have one.

I sat beside him on his bed and our parents called us for dinner. We put our things down and joined them at the table.

Our parents hilariously conversated with each other as though they didn't bury our grandparents in the backyard. Cameron became sick to his stomach, but he didn't bother to rush to a bathroom. Instead, he threw up in his food. Mother stood up and demanded he leave. I went into the kitchen, grabbed a roll of paper towels, and handed them to Cameron. He wiped his mouth and cleaned the area surrounding his plate. When he finished, he went upstairs and grabbed our belongings from his bedroom.

Father joined Cameron outside. He watched as he packed our things into the truck. When he pulled Cameron to him and hugged him. The hug caught him by surprise but for a moment it felt good. He thought maybe, just maybe our father loved him. Cameron smiled then father let go and smacked him hard as hell in the back of his head. Cameron was nearly bald; I knew that shit hurt him but not as much as everything else.

Chapter 9

Mother and I sat in silence at the table while Cameron waited for me in the car. Father rejoined mother and I at the table, well so I thought. He grabbed his plate and taken it into the living room and turned on the television. I stood up and told them the next time Cameron and I see them would be at their funerals. I then grabbed my plate and a soda from the refrigerator. When I walked past my parents to the front door, my father said to me "not if we kill you first." I took his words in and met Cameron in the car.

Cameron sped off and drove to Tony and his sister Lily's grandparents' place. Tony and Lily were eager to join us. Once inside the car Lily explained their grandparents had placed them on punishment for something they didn't do. Neither my brother nor I cared for their story. We had no place to live and although we had more than enough money, buying a place with no credit wasn't easy to do. Not only that our ages played a major role as well. For the first time in a while, I was depressed.

Cameron pulled over on the highway and I switched seats with him. After he slammed his door, I sped off and merged in traffic. I drove at a speed of one hundred miles an hour to William's house. We had to wait thirty minutes for William to shower and get dressed. I blasted music for him to hurry, shortly after he locked the front door behind him and got in the car. I looked at Cameron, it was the perfect time to make them prove their loyalty to us. Not only that it was the perfect time to form our crew and make a blood pack.

I drove to a gun store and parked the car. I turned around an gave Tony, Lily, and William a speech on loyalty. I told them if Cameron and I couldn't trust them they weren't allowed to hang with us. My brother then turned around and told them it was time for them to prove their loyalty and robbing a gun store was their first test. Lily and Tony were afraid, but William strangely was excited and ready as if he'd killed before. My brother even found it odd that his friend wasn't afraid. I leaned over Cameron and removed a pistol from the glovebox, I then turned around and handed it to William.

I went into my settings on my cellphone and set my alarm for ten minutes. I told them they had ten minutes to rob the store and get everything they needed. William was sarcastic towards me, he asked besides guns what else could they possibly need out of there. Cameron was going to answer but I stopped him by placing my hand over his mouth. He then laughed and I turned around and said to William "dumb ass besides guns you need to remove all video tapes." The store was flooded with cameras. I then said, "it usually takes me and Cameron five minutes to rob a store."

William left the car and went into the store while Lily and Tony stayed behind. Both myself and brother explained they couldn't allow William to execute the plan by himself, not that it wasn't possible, it was just that he would always have power over their heads. Lily and tony then ran into the store. We heard a gunshot; William shot the owner of the store in the ear. Lily stayed by the man's side while Tony helped William. William kicked the gun to Tony and Tony shot at a glass case for some of the rifles in the store. A fourth man in the back of the store heard all the commotion and called the police.

The man in the back hid under his desk in his office. William searched the back of the store and at first found no one. When he headed towards the front the man in his office backed out from under his desk and hit his head on his way out. William heard the loud thud and kicked down every door of the rooms in his presence until he found the man. The man was brought to the front of the store and shot. Tony had a bag of guns, he brought them outside and threw them in the back seat. Tony ran back in the store for William and Lily, the man William shot in the ear died.

Cameron and I heard the police sirens, but we didn't see them right away. I took Cameron's phone and called William. Soon as he answered he told me they knew they needed to get out of there, they were finishing some lose ends. I started the car and honked the horn. I then looked in my rearview mirror and saw the police. Lily, William, and Tony ran out the store and got in the car. I sped off in the opposite direction of the cops, a few cars continued in the direction of the gun store and three cops chased after us. I strongly felt it would be a long chase.

I drove at eighty miles an hour through red lights and oncoming traffic. William admitted he and tony dismembered the four men at the store and that they got the video tapes. Cameron comforted me while I drove. I got off the highway and took a detour. Two cops blocked one end of the street, I backed up and they sped up. I hit a mailbox once I was in the direction I needed to go. Cameron looked back at William, Lily, and Tony and told them he was satisfied with the way they executed the plan.

Apart from forgetting bullets for the guns I had to admit they did well. Cameron found one of my favorite CDs by the rapper Eminem and played it. I sped up to one hundred and twenty miles an hour when I turned the volume up. I made so many sharp turns the cops stopped chasing me. I slowed down and we laughed, we were relieved and surprised the chase ended early. I then drove to William's house where we hung out in the backyard for a few hours. We took the guns out the bag and played with them.

I took a pocket knife out and told everyone it was time for us to make our blood pack official. Me and Cameron no longer worked for our parents, we started a cult of our own. I went into the trunk of the car and retrieved a piece of paper out of one of my journals. I then found a pen and had everyone to write their whole names on the sheet of paper, I went last. I cut my right index finger and squeezed the blood onto the paper beside my name. My brother then went, then Tony, William, and Lily. I playfully snatched the knife from Lily and put it back in my pocket.

We stood in a circle and starred at the blood beside our names. I shouted out "this shit is fucking beautiful" and folded the paper. Before I put the paper in my pocket, I told them we had to decide on a leader. I asked them out of all of us which one of us could withhold the position. No one answered my question. I then told them we could all have an equal opportunity to win the position. Lily and Tony decided to stay at Williams. Meanwhile, Cameron rode with me to a gun range, we needed bullets.

I ran in the store and purchased many bullets needed for the handguns in our possession. The man turned the volume up on his television. I turned my head to the left and saw the highspeed chase, I took my change and receipt and left. When we arrived at William's place, we loaded all the guns. It was six-o-clock in the evening when we loaded the last one. I then asked William if he had any beer bottles. He went inside the trailer and came back minutes later with two large garbage bags of beer cans.

He told us his grandfather drank a lot every day as he poured the cans onto the grass. I then placed six cans onto a tree stomp and said, "the first person to shoot all six cans one after another will win the position as leader." Tony went first, he missed all the cans. William went after him, he shot two and missed the others. Cameron laughed maniacally and stepped up. He shot four and missed the last two. It was finally my turn.

Cameron had given me his rifle. I closed my right eye and pointed. Everyone cheered me on. I wanted them to stop, I couldn't focus. I yelled for them to stop, and they did. My hands shook as I starred at the cans out of one eye. I counted to ten and shot the first can. I repositioned myself and pointed again and shot the second, third, so on and so on.

Everyone cheered for me, my brother hugged me, and I high fived him. I was happy that I won the position. I was perfect for it. I starred at the sky and thought we needed a name for our crew. The question was proposed, everyone agreed we should have a name. Since there were five of us, I thought "Texas Five" was the perfect name for us. I suggested the name and they felt the same.

I dropped Lily and Tony at their grandparents. We arrived to them standing in the driveway yelling so loudly they woke some of their neighbors. I didn't park in the driveway, instead I dropped them off at the curb. I sped off before they could say goodnight. I stopped at a gas station on my way back to Williams. I went into the gas station and asked for thirty on pump number nine. I handed the cashier a fifty-dollar bill.

He took my money and didn't want to give me my change. I jumped over the counter, pistol whipped him, and took all the money out the register. The store manager and a few others called the police. I went into the back of the store and demanded the video tape; the woman had given me the tape without hesitation. The police arrived long after I left. I had time to still pump my gas and flirt with a few women.

By the time I got to Williams place he and my brother knew what I had done at the gas station.

I didn't deny what they already knew. I explained what happened at Tony and Lily's grandparents and what happened at the gas station. They told me they would've done the same thing if they were me. We played a few zombie video games and went to bed. During the night I went to the bathroom. I turned on the bathroom light and William's grandfather was passed out in the tub. I screamed for William; he followed my voice to the bathroom.

He told me to go back to bed, I told him I had to use the bathroom. William awakened his grandfather and bathed him. He helped him rewash his entire body. When finished he handed his grandfather a towel and he dried himself. Afterwards he stepped out the tub and William him to his bedroom. I closed the bathroom door, sat on the toilet, and peed. I then washed my hands, there were no paper towels in the bathroom.

I went to the kitchen, ripped a paper towel off the roll, and dried my hands. I turned on the television in the living room and slept in there for the remainder of the night. A little golden retriever puppy jumped on the couch. I didn't know they had a dog. I was too sleepy to play with the puppy. It fell asleep beside me. That morning I woke up, the puppy was on my back, I wiggled for him to move.

I showered and dressed for school. I went into the bedroom my brother and William slept in and awakened them. They showered, dressed for school, and ate a pop tart on their way out the house. When inside the car William went back into the trailer and asked his grandfather if he needed anything after school ended. His grandfather patted him on his back and said, "thank you my boy for checking on me, I love you dearly, I have everything I need." William hugged him and locked the front door behind him. He walked alongside the car to the end of the driveway and checked the mailbox, he pulled out so much mail we thought he hadn't checked it in weeks.

I drove us to school; we parted ways and went to class. Silvia blocked me from getting into my first period class. She was angry I didn't take her on that date as I promised. I told her I had a death in the family, which wasn't a lie. She comforted me and said, "whenever you need someone to talk to, you can call me, and I'll come running." In the little time I had known her, early on I could see she had a colorful personality. It was hard to resist her, and I loved girls who could speak Spanish and not only Spanish, other languages as well.

I leaned towards Silvia and kissed her gently on her lips. She held my face which I totally hated, but I gave her a pass since I liked her. I opened the door to my first period class and told her I'll add two shopping sprees to that dinner date Friday night. I then took her left hand, kissed it, then apologized. As she blushed, I went into my class and quietly closed the door behind me. My teacher marked me absent, I was five minutes late. I turned around and Silvia's face was pressed into the door, it was a bit creepy, but cute at the same time.

I sat in the only seat available in the back of the class. Everyone hated that seat; it was by far the worst seat in the school. The desk was disgusting. There were so many pieces of gum stuck under it and on top people could build a mountain out of it. The gum was molded, the odor was one I couldn't bear, it smelt like death back there. I was so far back I couldn't hear anything my teacher said, but it didn't matter. I was only there to turn in my assignments.

I looked out the only window in the back with me and saw my father. He held a sign that read "I'm going to kill all of you one by one." I wiped my eyes and double blinked, he wasn't there anymore. I stood up and the bell rang. I gathered my belongings and handed all my assignments to my teacher, she told me she was very proud of me. She added she would love it if I could come to class more. In response I said, "I wouldn't be able to complete all my assignments if I came to school more, having so much free time allows me to focus more."

I left first period and went to the bathroom. Jennifer, Janene, and Jessica were at the sinks doing their hair in the mirrors when I walked in. I closed my eyes, I didn't want to fight, I really had to pee. Their laughter ceased when I closed the door of the stall I went into. I pulled my pants down and sat on the toilet. I no longer had to pee, I had to do number two. They laughed as they heard my feces hit the water.

Embarrassed was an understatement and so was humiliated, words couldn't describe how I felt in that moment. I had no choice but to let go and give it to God. I reached for the tissue and looked up. Jennifer stood on the toilet in the stall to the right of me with her cellphone. She flashed as many pictures of me on the toilet wiping my ass as she could take. She stopped when her phone died. Janene and Jessica crawled mid-way under my stall and flashed a few pictures.

I reached in the toilet and threw some of my feces at Janene and Jessica. That got rid of them. Jessica called their dad to pick them up. I figured they wouldn't return for the remainder of the day. I washed my hands and went to my second period class. The girls' father was stuck at work, they waited for their mother in front of the school. A few students who ditched school saw them, they laughed at the shit smeared in Janene's hair and the shit smeared on Jessica's shirt.

Everyone who walked by them covered their noses. Their comments only angered the girls, people smelt them miles away. Forty-five minutes later their mother pulled in front of the school. The wide window in my second period allowed me to see everything. Their mother didn't want them to get in the car. They failed to tell her they were covered in shit. They cried and pleaded their cases, but their mother wouldn't listen.

Mrs. Jackson sped off leaving her girls in front of the school. Earlier that morning it rained; the wheels of her tires splashed them as she left. By then not only did the girls' smell like shit, but they also smelt like wet dog. They wiped their eyes and journeyed the five mile walk home. Me and a few others starred out the window until we could no longer see them. Our teacher blew a whistle. We bumped into each other on our way to our desks.

My cellphone vibrated a few times, I reached into my bra and answered it. Mr. Payne had an issue with it, but I stayed on the phone with my brother anyway. Cameron wanted me to meet him after class. Mr. Payne starred at me until the call ended. I chatted with Cameron for five minutes, we didn't talk about much. We goofed around until my teacher snatched my phone out my hand. He hung up in Cameron's face, I thought to myself how he shouldn't have done that.

Mr. Payne walked to the chalk board and threw my cellphone to me. I caught it and placed it in my right pocket. He proceeded with his lesson; a few students fell asleep. However, for the first time in a while I listened and took notes. After class I handed Mr. Payne more assignments that weren't due until finals. He smiled and grabbed assignments from other students. I ran to Cameron's class and waited for him in the hallway.

I explained what I thought I saw earlier to my brother. He told me my mind was playing tricks on me. He said it was normal, especially by the kind of man our father was. My brother had never spoken intelligently before, maybe school after all had an impact on him. I walked with him to the gymnasium, and we horse played our entire third period away. I got off my brother's back and went to the bleachers. I grabbed my backpack and ran to the cafeteria.

I ate lunch with Silvia and my brother joined us. He asked her if her sexy ass had a sister, she responded no. She went on and on about our date while my brother and I ate our lunches. He was a bit confused. He thought I had taken her out the week before. I couldn't remember whether I did or didn't. It didn't matter though; I was honored I was given another opportunity to take her out.

William, Tony, and Lily joined us for lunch. I introduced them to my girl as my crew. I told my crew whenever I wasn't around, they were to take care of the beautiful Ms. Jones. Silvia's cheeks were redder than a hot chili pepper. A fight broke out at the table behind us. Three girls jumped a guy. We pulled the girls off him and he ran.

The girls then informed us of what happened. Shortly after we let them go, he got caught dating the three sisters. Me and Lily had taken our treys to the garbage. The others cleaned the table behind us. We parted ways. I walked Silvia to her class and went to mines. I didn't realize how much I had eaten. I was full as hell once I got to my fourth period class, I sat down and fell asleep.

Chapter 10

After class, students were in the hallway on their cellphones laughing. Cameron called me and told me why they were laughing. I snatched a guy's phone and saw the YouTube video my enemies posted of me on the toilet wiping my ass. They added special affects to the video. The video then showed me naked on the toilet, wiping my ass, and sniffing it. I handed the guy his phone and met my brother. Together we searched for the sisters.

We found the girls in principal Jenkins's office. I locked the door behind me and demanded they take the video down. They wouldn't comply. High as usual, principal Jenkins sat there and did nothing. I checked his pulse, I had to make sure he was still breathing. He threw me off guard for a minute sitting there not blinking, not speaking, and probably not thinking. I looked at the girls, I couldn't focus on him anymore.

I pushed Jessica out the way and turned on the intercom. I told all the students Jennifer Jackson, Janene Jackson, and Jessica Jackson had been bitten by a coyote and they had rabies. Jennifer snatched the speaker, and I broke it. They weren't going to torment me anymore. Surprisingly, principal Jenkins stood up and shoved the girls out his office. It was about time he did something I said a loud. He slammed the door and told us he knew exactly what he was doing.

We laughed and hugged our principal. My crew already knew what my heart desired most, and so did Principal Jenkins. He wrote down the name of the bar they usually hung out at on a regular. I thanked him and grabbed the paper. Lily googled searched the bar and found the address on her cellphone. My crew followed me to the car. I drove to a costume store.

The friendly store manager helped us find wigs that suited us and a police uniform and shoes. The uniforms were perfect, especially mines. The name on my uniform read "Johnson". Johnson was my last name, and I was officer Johnson. We thanked the manager and approached the cashier. I handed a grand to the tall shy gentleman and left. I ran the plan by everyone, and no one had any objections.

All we needed was a cop car, I contacted principal Jenkins. He gave us the address of one of his friends who was the sheriff. We met Sheriff King, had a cup of coffee, and he handed me the keys to his car. I then handed him a couple grand to not rat us out. I drove the squad car while Tony, William, and Lily rode with my brother to the bar. We parked and me and Cameron went inside. We approached the manager, I told him we received many complaints from the bar of three teenagers.

The manager pointed, me and Cameron turned around and saw the girls. I took out my handcuffs while Cameron pointed his gun at them. We watched them arguing with a bartender. Cameron cocked his gun and they turned around. They froze, I handcuffed them. They wouldn't shut up, Cameron hit Janene in her eye, that shut all of them up. We walked them to the squad car and placed them in the backseat.

I drove the squad car to William's house and Cameron trailed me. William, Lily, and Tony pulled the girls out the car and pushed them down a hill behind William's house. They were still handcuffed on their way down, two of them broke their arms. William ran into his house and retrieved three cages. The cages belonged to old dogs he had when he was younger. He threw the cages down the hill. I lit a cigarette, pulled out a knife, and we all proceeded down the hill towards the girls.

I reached the bottom of the hill first. I pulled Jennifer by her hair and shoved her into one of the cages. Cameron and Tony placed Janene and Jessica in their cages when they reached the bottom. They screamed and screamed, I threatened them. I told them if they didn't stop, I would feed them a part of themselves. Thankfully, they stopped. I then ordered Lily to find us some tape.

Lily ran up the hill to William's house and found a roll of duct tape. At the edge of the hill, she slid the tape down to us. I picked it up and ripped off a few pieces. William opened the cages; we went inside and taped the girls' arms and legs. We left their mouths untapped so they could talk. They had no idea who we were. I removed my wig and their eyes widened.

I assumed they knew who we were, but they didn't. The others removed their wigs and Cameron removed his mustache. After Lily revealed herself, I'm sure the girls realized the woods would be their tomb. My crew sat on a log while I removed a patch of Jessica's hair with my knife. As she screamed, I informed the girls why we kidnapped them. They begged us not to kill them. I placed tape around their heads covering their mouths.

We granted the girls their last wish. We didn't murder them, we left them for dead. I kneeled in front of the cages and said, "we'll see all of you in hell." We ran up the hill, had a few beers, and went grocery shopping. We bought steaks, ribs, crabs, and fish. I drove us back to Williams where he cooked dinner for us. We had stuffed crab with a bottle of champagne.

We set up our tents and gathered around a campfire. We sat in lawn chairs eating marshmallows. Cameron looked at his phone, there was a message from dad. He switched seats with Lily and sat by me. The message read "your mother has decided to start a new career as a singer". A few seconds later another message followed with an address and the date of her performance. We dismissed our father messages and enjoyed the rest of the night.

The next morning, my inbox was flooded with messages from our parents. Our father wanted us to join him for our mother's performance. Of course, we had no intentions of going after the way they discarded our grandparents, but we told him we would meet him Friday night. We had three days to think about it. Cameron woke up the others. We showered and dressed for school. Upon our arrival, me and Cameron met with Principal Jenkins.

He was thrilled to know we executed the plan with ease. We sat down and I handed him another grand for all his help. He then handed it back to me, I asked him why he wouldn't accept the money. He sighed and told us him and his wife had stolen a kilo of coke from his brother. His brother was a notorious gangster/drug dealer. He was well-known in the south, and it was a matter of time before he realized his dope was missing. I handed him the money again and told him he could always count on us as along as we could count on him.

Cameron walked to the mini refrigerator and grabbed a few beers for us. We skipped all our classes that day and kicked it. We told principal Jenkins we had nowhere to live. In response he told us he knew a real estate agent that could help us. He took our full names and phone numbers; he would have the realtor give us a call. I threw away my beer cans and went to the bathroom. I sat on the toilet and looked out the window.

Once again, I thought I saw my father. I wiped my eyes and hurried out the bathroom in fear. I expressed to

Cameron what I saw. He helped me to my chair. Principal Jenkins handed me a bottle of water, I splashed some of it on my face. Cameron took the rest from me and drank it. I leaned back in my chair and stared at the ceiling. Principal Jenkins pulled out a deck of cards.

I never played poker before. Principal Jenkins taught me the game. I told myself if I ever went to Vegas I would play. It took me a while to understand the game. Once I understood I was unstoppable. I betted Cameron ten grand I could beat him. He accepted my bet.

We played six rounds; I won every game. I placed the cards back in its box and handed them to Principal Jenkins. Before we left his office, he gave us his brother's address. I took it and placed it in a pocket on my jacket. I then reminded him we needed housing; he remembered. Cameron slapped our principal's hand and walked out. I followed him out.

Cameron and I waited for our crew in the car in front of the school. Fifteen minutes passed and we saw them. I honked the horn, and they ran to us. Cameron reached for the address in my pocket. He plugged it into google maps and I followed the GPS. Three hours later we arrived at the address. I parked down the street.

We had to blend in. The neighborhood had five notorious drug dealers. Their names were Big Al, Jose', Ronnie Mac, and Frostbite. Cameron checked the house out. He ran back to the car and informed me all five dealers were in the spot. They only sold drugs out the house, nothing more and nothing less. Their trap house was always jumping.

They always had many customers. What separated them from most drug dealers was they never cut any of their supply with anything, their drugs were pure. Cameron and I got out the car. I stole a dog from a neighbor's front yard; we blended in. The pit bill of course was aggressive, but we managed to control it. Once in front of the house Cameron took the dog. We approached the front door.

We didn't have to knock or ring the doorbell. The door was already open. There were so many people to push through but we got a good scope of the place. In the living room we saw all five dealers. Early on it was clear who was in charge. From that alone we knew who's house it was. The house belonged to Frostbite, and Frostbite was Principal Jenkin's brother.

Frostbite wasn't his real name, but he preferred it. He got the nickname when he was a teenager. At thirteen he sold more drugs than anyone. People referred to him as the coldest in the name and because of that his father nicknamed him Frostbite. We stood in line and waited our turn. There were twenty people in front of us. Thirty minutes later it was finally our turn.

Cameron and I approached Frostbite and his people. We bought a little bit of everything. For some odd reason Frostbite liked us and invited us to stay a while. We watched him serve thousands of junkies, literally my eyes hurt. We couldn't leave before killing them. If we had of Frostbite most definitely would have killed his brother and wife. Four hours passed and we hadn't moved off the couch.

Cameron fell asleep while I played games on my cellphone. Frostbite realized we were bored and handed us some dope. He allowed his boys to take a break and taught us the game, well so he thought. We weren't strangers to the dope game. Cameron and I knew exactly how it worked. Our parents sold drugs most of our lives, they stopped a week they forced us into the cult. An hour in Frostbite and his boys was impressed.

They were impressed so much they invited us to work for them for two months. I rejected their offer; they raised their weapons at us. Frostbite forced everyone out his house and had his boys tie us up. Big Al put a knife to Cameron's throat and threatened him not to blink. If he blinked Big Al would cut him. He stared at the wall in front of him until his eyes watered. The boys were shocked he hadn't blinked yet.

Frostbite and his boys were careless individuals. They failed miserably at watching us. He should've had one of his boys sit by us and watch us closely. Their cellphones constantly rang, they were more focused on the money than they were of us. My brother still hadn't blink and I had more than enough time to retrieve my pocketknife. I had it between my fingers and cut through my tape and his tape. When Frostbites call ended, he approached us.

Cameron blinked and Big Al cut him on his face. Cameron then took his knife and stabbed him in the forehead. Big Al fell backwards, and the others ran towards us. When Ronnie Mac got close enough to me, I shoved the knife in his abdomen. He bled out and died. Frostbite tested his luck; he pointed a gun at us. We stared into the eye of the pistol.

He took too long to shoot it, I snatched it and shot him and Jose who hid behind the couch. Cameron and I grabbed all the money and drugs. I went into the kitchen and found a couple of heavy-duty garbage bags. I ran back into the living room and handed Cameron one. He threw all the money inside his bag, and I threw the many bags of dope into mines. We doubled checked the house for any extras and found a trunk of men's' jewelry. I ran outside and I saw a few junkies passed out in the front yard.

I hurried down the street to the car. I drove mid-way down the street until I reached Frostbites house. I ran inside and Cameron ran out with the two bags. I went back inside for the trunk of jewelry, but it was too heavy for me to carry alone. I plopped down on the couch and waited for Cameron. After he shoved the second bag into the backseat two of the junkies had awakened. Cameron forced them away from the house.

Cameron ran inside and helped me lift the truck. Our strength was no match for the trunk, it was too heavy. I looked out the front door and saw a man who might've been a bodybuilder. I ran outside and asked for his help. He didn't want to help us at first but when I had given him some money his attitude changed. He followed me inside and helped us lift it to the car. He dropped his end when we were close enough to it.

I let the trunk go and opened the right back door. The man sat his end on the seat and Cameron pushed it inside. I then ran back to the house and slammed the front door. When I turned around the man was in my face. I pushed him; he missed all three steps. He jumped up quickly and wiped himself odd as if he didn't fall. Cameron laughed from the passenger seat of the car.

The man held on to the driver door, the window was down. I started the car, and the windows automatically went up. The window caught his hand. I started the car and drove off. The window hadn't taken his hand off yet, he held on. I sped up; his right arm was ripped off. People in the neighborhood saw what happened but did nothing to help the man.

We were focused on so many things at once we hadn't noticed William, Lily, and Tony were no longer in the car. Cameron called Tony and asked where they were. They told us they were tired; they took a Lyft to Williams house. William then took the phone from Tony and told us he wanted us to take him to see his mother who was prostitute.

98

Cameron was hesitant on taking him to see his mother, she was suicidal. She tried to kill herself in front of them on their last visit with her. Days later she was hospitalized for depression.

The three-hour journey back to William's house left my right shoulder sore. I rested for an hour before we took William to see his mother. In that time Cameron hoped he changed his mind, but he never did. Lily and Tony stayed at the house and supposedly went to bed, so they say. The pain in my shoulder hadn't ceased. Cameron didn't want to drive but I forced him. The abandoned warehouse Williams mothers usually slept in was vacant.

We searched the streets for his mother, for a while we couldn't find her. Just as we were leaving William spotted a shoe. He was certain his mother wore those shoes often. William ran to the shoe and picked it up. He then spotted the second one behind the dumpster. Traces of blood was found on the back of it. William began to panic.

Me and Cameron searched a couple alleys nearby the dumpster. We didn't find anything. We ran to William and saw him inside the dumpster. He told us the smell was awful. After all it was a dumpster, but William made it clear the smell was more than garbage. We watched him throw trash in every direction for a few minutes. Then something caught his attention.

Printed in the USA
CPSIA information can be obtained
at www.ICGtesting.com
LVHW080802040823
754031LV00015B/841